A SECOND LIFE WORTH LIVING

KAREN LUCIA

1

My body ached. Every inch. Every fiber. Every bone. It all rang out as the air pressure shifted with the weather. The roil of clouds. The flashes of lightning and whipping winds.

Nobody told me my second life would hurt so much. Considering how I died the first time around, maybe I shouldn't have been surprised. It's not easy to come back from having every bone in one's body broken.

Kea would tell me I was being dramatic. I would have told her that even if it wasn't every bone, it had come pretty damn close. And besides, that didn't account for the bullets either. Not to mention the crushed esophagus. Those wounds had been no small triviality.

I suppressed a groan as my once cracked bones creaked. Sinking deeper into the mire, I played dead. Not a hard sell since I already had one foot in the grave. Still, the last thing I wanted was to be caught. I could always die again. Maybe the next time would be permanent. I could only hope. I couldn't imagine the pain of two deaths lingering on this body.

The sniffers padded closer and I held my breath. I kept my eyes open, but my stare distant and empty. I knew the look of the dead well. I felt the rapidly cooling hands of the recently deceased butting against my own as the sniffer nosed through the heap.

If I weren't so scared of discovery, I would have wondered how many of my fellow deceased would come back as I had. How many of the sea of bodies around me would be subjected to a second life, and how would they choose to spend it?

I had done nothing with mine. Squandered it maybe. Lived the same inane existence as my first life. Worse, I wasn't even a contributing member of society anymore, too scared to return to work. Too scared to leave my apartment most days. My nerves had kept me locked in my unit for a week straight already. I hadn't even noticed the days passing until the snacks ran out and I was forced to pull myself off the couch. My death had brought on an ambivalence that had well and truly ended my life, succeeding where the beatings and the noose had failed.

Right up until I found myself here, laying in a field of bodies as a sniffer drew closer, seeking the living.

I could hear the chopping breath of a survivor struggling to hold on to life somewhere nearby. I could hear the shouts of another as they were hauled off for interrogation, torture, and death. Would they come back vengeful, their bones aching and skin itching from the damage done to them in life? Would they come back, a noose still around their neck? To struggle and gasp and fight for life once again, only to die their second death as I nearly had?

I hadn't even done anything wrong to die a first time. My crime had been being in the wrong place at the wrong time, getting me wrangled up with a swarm of abolitionists. After a while, even my interrogator decided I had done nothing wrong. Nothing ever, in fact. After only a moment of debate, the shades decided I couldn't get them information. I would make a terrible informant. That at the very least, I was a good prop for a public example. All I was when the shades dragged my tortured and broken body out into the streets was a puppet suitable only to die.

One would think that thought would get a person fired up. Make them vengeful. Make them spiteful at the very least. Make a person think *maybe I shouldn't be as useless now as I was then*. Try to prove their murderers wrong by living a full and hearty second life rife with intrigue and wonder. Instead, I was laying in mud, surrounded by the bodies of actual interesting people as a sniffer nosed me over, not even registering my existence.

Thank whatever god was out there that their mechanical noses hadn't yet been tuned to the morbid scent of whatever wild magic kept me kicking.

The sniffer nosed the survivor taking in ragged breaths and snarled.

I remained still, ignoring the drive to blink. Ignoring the icy drizzle that coated my skin and sank through my clothes. Ignoring the stench of death all around.

"What do you say?" The two trench coated officers considered the man at their feet as their sniffer continued its warning growl. Not a dog anymore. Not quite. Not the way they had been bred, trained, modified.

The shorter of the two nudged the wounded man with his boot, shifting the rifle slung over his shoulder. "Nah. Look at that wound. Put him down."

A moment later, a gunshot exploded nearby and the ragged breathing stopped. A fresh swath of warm blood pooled over my hand.

The sniffer move on. The officers moved on. I stared at the sky, watching as the rain started once again, releasing freezing drops down onto us. Feeling the wet ooze of another man's blood between my fingers, I wondered, not for the first time in my lives, how the hell I had ended up here. What luck did I have that always put me where I ought not to be?

How many others in this cold, damp mire

had been caught where they hadn't intended? The river bottoms were a common enough weekend spot, even after the rains. I felt like one minute it had been me, dogs, families, couples, and the next there had been a frenzied rush as abolitionists from the recent march sought escape in the wooded park, the river; fleeing in every direction but toward the gunfire.

The day had been chill, wet, and dreary, but it had also been calm. Then it had been anything but.

Somewhere to my right, a fight broke out; shouts, cries of pain, gunshots. I stayed still. I didn't do anything except dread the stiffness setting into my muscles and the ache in my bones. It's not like I could do anything to help, anyway. I wasn't a brawler. I was unarmed. Even if I wasn't, I didn't know how to shoot straight. I would just be a liability in a fight. Besides, my first death had taught me exactly how mortal my body was. Had taught me how little pain I could actually endure before screaming, resorting to begging and pleading with snot dripping from my nose and spittle on my lips. Bennet Smith was no great specimen of courage, it turned out.

The gunfire cracked and popped and fizzled out. I could only assume which side had won, but really there was never any question which side would win this struggle in the end.

All the abolitionists hoped to accomplish was a blaze of gory glory that stood a thin chance of sparking a full-scale revolution. I knew better. Most of the population was happy to stay at status quo. Don't fuck with the government and they won't fuck with you. As long as you weren't caught in the wrong place at the wrong time, anyway.

I lay there, thinking about what cruel twist of magic had decided to bring me back to live out this miserable, mud-covered life. How unlucky did I have to be to be caught in the crossfire between the abolitionists and the authorities not once, but twice? If I got shot here, would that be it? Or would I come back again with another ache to complain about when it rained?

The blood running over my hand had since started to cool. The life in the area dwindled as abolitionist and innocent bystander alike were hauled off or shot where they lay, crawled, or begged for aid.

The sniffers wouldn't find me. That gave me solace. Their sight was one of magic. The beasts could only detect the truly living. That didn't mean an officer couldn't step on my gut and elicit a response that showed just how aware I was, or look down and see me blink.

My survival instincts kept me still, ignoring the ache, ignoring the cries for help. Ignoring the blood and mud and bodies around me.

In the back of my mind, I knew Kea was right. I was a coward hiding behind the excuse of survival. Where had my survival instincts gotten me before? Nowhere good. Left broken, hanged, dead. It had only been Kea risking her life to steal my body away that had saved me. She had come just in time to greet me back into this second life as I kicked and floundered and groped at the rope choking my new life out of me.

Maybe she would have stood up and joined the fight had she been here. She certainly would not have gone down without throwing a few fists first. No doubt she would have survived, escaped, brought a few others with her in a valiant rescue. I was not Kea.

Rain poured over my face. I let my eyes close. I wouldn't be leaving this muck anytime soon.

2

I was wet and cold and ready for a shower when I finally climbed out of the river bottoms. Covered in mud and the blood of others, I knew better than to take any main roads home. In the middle of a city as coated in cement and neon as Zenith, there were few enough green spaces, and fewer that boasted as much mud and mire as I was coated in. The shades would be fast to bundle me up and spirit me away if they saw my condition. Then the torture would start again. The questions. The realization that I was still, once again, completely and utterly useless. Would Kea even bother trying to recover my body this time? Probably not. I wouldn't.

I hurried. Eyes constantly on the move. A nervous glance over my shoulder at every corner. I was the picture of a suspicious character, but there wasn't any stopping my anxiety's manifestation. It was only when the familiar cracks in the walls of my lackluster building came into view that my pulse slowed enough for me to realize I hadn't even succeeded in getting the snacks that had driven me from the obscurity of my home. There was probably a can hidden in the back of the cupboard to sustain me until morning.

I climbed up to my apartment. My fingers fished around in my muck filled pocket for my keys, glad for the dingy lighting of the hallway and the overall lack of shits given by the complex owner to maintain the cleanliness of the shared spaces. My muddy tracks would just blend with the last set dragged in by my neighbors. I found my key and wiped the dirt off with the cleanest part of my shirt I could find before unlocking my door and stepping into the silent refuge of my tiny apartment.

Mine was an old building, built in the days before Zenith had been called Zenith. Before the influx of mega-corporations drove growth, and growth drove the city to rapidly expand. Before the collection of towns had been consumed by the sprawl of the city, wiping their existence from the map. It was a wonder the relic hadn't been knocked down yet to make way for another high-rise.

The pipes rattled and clanked when I turned on the water, but soon enough the liquid started pouring from the shower head. I still let it run a few moments as I stripped off my filthy clothing before risking stepping in. This wasn't luxury, but at least the water still got hot in this building. Well, at least it got hot if you timed your showers right. That wasn't the case everywhere I had lived in the past. I didn't need much in the way of creature comforts. I never had.

The hot water was not enough to soothe my joints nor warm my muscles, but it was a step in the right direction. Nothing could really take away the images lodged in my mind. The bodies of children caught in the crossfire. The government wasn't doing itself any favors in bringing the masses over to their side in their bid to maintain control, but the media would be too scared to show what had actually transpired today. It was all too easy to say that the violent abolitionists had stormed into the park brandishing weapons and shouting about reform when the real heroes had arrived in a hale of bullets. Whether that hale of bullets had been discerning or not would be a question for a different day.

When the water finally ran clear, I shut off the shower and stood dripping. The waste of water seemed an egregious offense on top of all that had already transpired. This world had enough problems without me adding to them. But I knew the reality was that nothing I did mattered. Nothing on an individual scale would ever amount to anything. The big corps, industry, government; they all needed to get in line and get in league with the needs of the populace. Considering the carnage of the day, that wasn't likely to happen anytime soon.

I dried myself off, pulled on a pair of boxers

so I wouldn't get any more complaints from the voyeurs across the alley, turned the television to some mindless feel good game show, and sank into my couch. My head fell back, and I drifted off to the soothing sounds of slapstick comedy and boxed laughter.

3

I didn't want to go out, but Kea wasn't to be denied. She never was. When I had hemmed and hawed when she called, in full Kea fashion, she had shown up at my door and all but muscled me out of my apartment amidst claims that it was all for my health and wellbeing. She had at least given me the good graces to allow me to dress myself, even if she did frown at my secondhand hoodie with its moth-eaten holes. Who was I trying to impress? If anything, I wanted to be as inconspicuous as possible. It wasn't a hard sell. Brown hair, a light beard, a completely generic face in a city filled with generic faces.

The only problem with my plan to blend in was Kea. Kea and her toned muscles and perfectly coifed red hair. Kea and her charisma. Kea and her wellspring of charm. It was easy to get lost behind her, but people still took the moment to look at her companion, and even that brief moment of attention was more than I wanted.

They had broadcast my face before I was hung. They had dragged me out, legs no longer able to support me from all the damage, face bloodied and bruised. Propped me up and pulled a hood over my head after making proclamations of my alleged crimes against the state. I hadn't heard a single one, barely alive as I was at that moment before death. The rope had been secured and I had dropped.

But for that moment before the hood, my face had been shown to the country. Even wrecked as it was from the weeks in captivity, Kea had recognized me. Generic and unimpressive and suddenly plastered everywhere. A martyr of the revolution I had no interest in being a part of. Painted as a devious enemy of the state.

I dug my hands into my pockets and followed Kea out of my building while she grumbled about the state of the structure, telling me I needed to get my landlord to put in the time to clean the place up. Commenting on the muddy tracks on the ratty carpets and the dust bunnies in the hallways.

I muttered something about getting right on that, then pulled my hood up as we took to the streets.

Kea was a force. One I had always clung to the coattails of in childhood. She should have left me in her dust long ago, but she continued to drag me along behind her. Like today, her arm linked through mine to guide me through the city as though she thought I was likely to turn and run if she left me to my own devices. I probably would. Drop off the back of our walk, slip into the crowd, and turn for home. The idea was intoxicating. A pair of comfy boxers, sprawled out on the couch with a bag of chips and a beer.

As if she could sense my thoughts, Kea's arm tightened on mine and she yanked me into our usual place. She sat me down at our usual table and fixed me with her usual glare that told me that if I tried to run for home, she would catch me, throw me over her shoulder, and drag me right back to my seat. Then she smiled and strode to the bar, exchanging words with a few of the other patrons as she passed. I had never tested her, but I was certain she had the muscles to make good on her threats. Built, beautiful, and with no self-restraint. I sighed, set my elbows on the table and resigned myself to trying to have a good time.

Kea set a beer in front of me and pulled back my hood. I exhaled through my nose but left my hood off. It wasn't likely I would be recognized from the broadcast, and from Kea's report, the state hadn't released my name when murdering me. That was my saving grace, at least. I had still lost my job for the weeks of absence, but to the world, Bennet Smith was still alive and hirable. If I could bring myself to get off my couch and put on pants long enough to hold any of those jobs down. It all just seemed like a bit too much effort to have to put in just now.

"So... You plan on moping about for the rest of your life, or do I get my friend back at some point?" Kea asked.

I shrugged and drank.

She sighed and sat back in her chair. "Well, I guess this isn't too far off from what you were like before." Her eyes drifted to the screen behind me. If it was playing the same station as the one to our left, her eyes had fixed on the news. I studied the rising bubbles in my beer.

"There was another shootout," Kea said, her face set in a deep frown.

"At the river bottoms?" I asked, not bothering to look at the screen. The news was never good these days. If it wasn't a fluff piece, I didn't want it.

"Yeah." She looked back to me. "You heard about it already?"

"I was trying to enjoy a walk outside."

"You were there?" Her eyes widened. "Oh shit, the mud. You know that's not fair to the other tenants, you leaving your muddy tracks everywhere." She chided. "What did you do?"

"What did I do when?"

"At the river bottoms. When the shooting started."

I shrugged, setting down my now mostly empty glass. She signaled for another.

"Well, when the shooting started, and I

realized running wasn't going to get me anywhere but dead, I did the next best thing and hid. I spent hours in a pile of corpses while shades and sniffers made their way through, picking off the dying and harvesting the useful." I emptied my glass. A bitter note had crept into my voice in anticipation of a scolding.

"You didn't fight back?"

"I'm sorry, I thought you knew me better than that," I sniped sarcastically.

She shook her head, a grumble in her throat that I couldn't hear in the din of the bar, but I knew was there. It had been a stupid question on her part. Of course I hadn't fought. Of course she would have. She let it drop.

We sat in silence for a long moment. There was nothing uncommon about that. We had practically been attached at the hip through our childhood. There was no need to fill every silence between us. Still, this particular silence felt just a touch oppressive, her great disappointment in me emanating off of her in waves.

I studied my fingernails, flicking flecks of missed dirt from my nail beds.

My empty was swapped for a full, which I downed half of in one swig. I wouldn't say I was coping well with my re-entry into life. The thing that really burned was that nobody seemed to have noticed I was gone. Well, except Kea, and my ex-employer.

I looked up from the grave dirt still darkening my nails. In a hunt for any distraction from my dark thoughts and the memory of my boots swinging helplessly beneath me, my eyes fell on Rhapsody. She wasn't just any distraction. She was the distraction I had been silently pining after for longer than I cared to admit.

My eyes fell from her perfect curves and waves of brown hair to the corner where her beau liked to hang out, conspicuously trying to look inconspicuous as he kept tabs on her while she worked. Strangely, today her handsome goon of a boyfriend was missing.

"Why don't you take a chance for once and ask her to grab a drink?" Kea knew full well what held my attention without even bothering to follow my eyes.

"Nobody wants to fuck a corpse," I groused to my beer, pretending there was no slur to my voice after only one.

"Well, I mean, that's not entirely true, but we do want to avoid those people," Kea said lightly, and not helpfully. She turned serious. "Besides, you are not a corpse. You are alive."

"What do you call it when a person is living in the same body they died in?"

"People do that all the time. Go down, somebody does some chest compressions, and *viola*, they are back among the living in the same body they died in."

My finger rimmed my mug. "I feel like this a bit different and you know it. I'm just a walking cadaver."

She rolled her eyes and forced me to look at her. "Are you really going to live your second life like you lived your first? Never taking a risk? Never trying anything new? What a waste." She crossed her arms and leaned back, kicking a boot up onto the table, precariously balanced on two legs of her chair. "From what I know of you, Second Lifes: your heart beats, your blood pumps, your lungs take in oxygen and expel CO_2. You can be killed all over again. That sounds like life to me."

"And I'm wasting it."

"You said it." She smirked and downed her beer. "If you don't ask her, I will."

"For me?"

She laughed heartily. "What do you think?"

I glowered, knowing full well what she had meant. Kea was the charmer I could never be.

She popped an eyebrow, waiting.

"Fine," I groused. Good idea or bad, I finished off my beer and stood. Then sat and fell into a drunken pout.

With a roll of her eyes, Kea stood and moved to the bar. I watched her, drunk with envy as she leaned against the bar, a smirk the picture of seduction on her lips, and ordered two more beers.

4

"You wanna drink me?" I slurred drunkenly, foolishly leaning on my liquid courage as heavily as I leaned against the bar. "No." I held up a hand. "You wanna grab me drink you? No… Nevermind," I said, giving up to sulk over my lifetimes of poor decisions.

It was late. Too late for me to still be out. Too late to stop myself from making a complete ass of myself.

"Perhaps you have had enough," Rhapsody suggested sympathetically. The grin on her lips held amusement and a touch of pity. It made my heart fall into my stomach.

"Yes, yes. I had enough." I looked at Kea. She could drink me under the table. She could get anybody she wanted any night she wanted. She could win any brawl she got into. I was wickedly jealous of the woman.

Kea laughed, and I frowned. It wasn't fair to her to be peeved at her outgoing nature, her innate ability to draw others to her.

"You disappeared a few months back. Didn't think I would see you again, honestly," Rhapsody said, leaning across the bar, bringing my slippery attention back to her.

I returned my eyes to her, confused.

"You used to come in here with Kea a lot," she said, nodding toward my friend. "Didn't leave with her a lot of the time, but not many can drink the bar closed like she can."

Damn outgoing, iron livered Kea. I swallowed, pushing back my jealousy. It was a vile trait, and I sought its source to address it. Kea and I had been opposites since childhood. She was always willing to take a risk. To stand up and shake a stick at anybody she didn't agree with. To flirt and grin and get on with anybody who struck her fancy. I always did what I was doing now: sat, and watched, and envied.

"Went away for a little," I said evasively, my drunkenness subsiding slightly at the memory of my own death. My voice was quiet, and I considered the contents of my empty mug, then raised my eyes to Rhapsody. "Back now."

"I see that."

"Didn't think I would be."

She sat back. "Well, I'm glad you are, even if I am cutting you off." With a sigh, she pressed back to her feet, leaned over and grabbed my empty mug with a wink.

I watched her in utter confusion.

5

Another night. Another pair of boxers. Another mindless game show playing on the television. I was just glad that Kea was taking the night easy and hadn't forced me into pants and out to the bar with her again. I think she knew that with the weather cold and rainy as it was, I would be in a sour mood as my bones creaked through the city and had let me have my trash TV for the night.

She finished rummaging through my cupboards, returning to the couch, baring the fruits of her hunt: a stale bag of chips. She tossed a blanket onto my lap with a disgusted shake of her head. I hadn't been as attentive to my spread as I could have been. Fair enough. I didn't want to see my best friend's junk either. She settled in beside me, shaking the bag of chips as she gazed into its depths as though there was some secret hiding in there.

"I know you don't want to go throwing yourself right back into the working world, but it may be a nice change of pace for you to get a job. Get you out of this apartment at least." She selected an undamaged specimen of a chip and popped it into her mouth whole.

"I got out last week, remember? Went to the river bottoms, almost got shot to hell. Hid in a pile of corpses. Seems like plenty 'getting out' to me," I said bitterly, eyes on the flashing nonsense gracing the screen in front of us.

She ignored my snappishness. "Even if you don't want to go back to wasting away in an office, there's a mini mart hiring down the street. Or there are plenty of barista positions open. Didn't you used to do that while you were in school?" She asked, as if we didn't know every intimate detail of each other's lives. When I didn't answer, she prodded. "Might at least get you some money so you can take Rap out on a nice date."

I laughed. "As if. She's got that guy. Mister Handsome."

"Meatpants Magee has been out of the picture for a few months. Rhapsody is freelance right now. You really should ask her out."

"As if I could hold a candle to Mister Meatpants," I groused. "Average in every way and completely uninteresting."

"One, don't be so mean to my best friend. Bennet Smith is great. Two, Rap dumped Meatpants. Three, she was asking after you yesterday."

I didn't believe her. "It would just be a waste of both our time. I wouldn't be able to hold her attention long."

"I mean, let's be real. You've been killed before. In some circles, that could be considered interesting. Or exciting. Or something outside the norm."

"I can't exactly talk about that with her."

Kea shrugged. "Well, maybe not on the first date…"

"So, I'll put it on the list for if I make it to the second or third date," I muttered.

"You could try a little confidence."

I rolled my eyes and fluffed the blanket over my legs. "I have nothing to offer. The only exciting things that have ever happened to me were pure coincidence. A mindless decision to stand here rather than there. I don't do anything exciting."

"You don't choose to, no," Kea agreed. "You prefer staying in your little bubble of contrived ignorance. It's not safety or peace you have in there with you. It's fantasy. Do you think I plot out every exciting twist and turn to my life? I don't. I just go out and live the life I've been given. Good, bad, shitty, worse. You gotta do something with it. One would think you, of all people, would know that." She brandished her chip bag at me. "You had a shit life before. Do you really think doing the same thing over again is going to result in a different outcome?"

"You thought I had a shit life?"

She frowned. "That's not what I meant."

With a shake of her head, she backpedaled. "No, it's exactly what I meant. You had a shit life. Boring. Inane."

"Comfortable. Safe."

"Lonely."

I drew in air through my nose and failed to think of a rebuttal.

"You were lonely. You still are. Because you never take a chance. And you can't tell me you were safe when I literally watched you get dragged out and hanged for dissidence you had no part in." Her voice cracked ever so slightly. She stood and set her back to me as she took a steadying breath. She shifted through her bag of chips again in a bid to disguise the swell of pain.

I sat up straighter, glaring at her back. "So I should grab a gun? Start fighting the man? Demand reform? Shout for freedom? Join the revolution?"

She turned, a glower on her face as she tossed the bag of chips into my lap and blew out a long exhale. She leaned over, a beefy mitt supporting her against the back of my dingy couch. "You should do anything at all. Get off this couch. Put some fucking pants on. Do anything. I don't care if all you decide to do is walk to the fucking ice cream shop and get something other than vanilla or chocolate or whatever inane flavor you always order. Make a decision. Any decision. Challenge yourself.

Step out of that shitty little box you call existence and live. You got a second chance. Not everybody does. Not everybody will."

I rolled my eyes and set the chips on the coffee table. "Are you coming to terms with your own mortality, Kea? Is that what this is?"

She growled and straightened. "Fuck you." She even stomped her foot. "Do you have any idea what I went through watching you get hanged? Do you have any idea what I felt watching you die? I didn't want to make your death about me, but since you are such an ever-loving shithead, I will. The relief I felt when I cut you down, kicking and fighting for life... I..." She rounded on me again. "Fuck. You." She jabbed a finger at me.

"Fuck me," I agreed. "I'm sorry I let you down. I'm exactly the same as I was before. Maybe shittier. Turns out dying doesn't make a person bouncy and fun. Turns out getting shot and tortured and killed fucking sucks. Turns out coming back from having your body broken means you get to feel every point of mending when you do the simplest task. When there's a little change in the air. When you shift position just slightly. I didn't ask for this. I never would have wanted this."

"Well, you fucking have it." She said, her voice more subdued once again, but her temper still hot. "Do you really intend to spend it watching other people guess what minor celebrity is dancing around in a costume?"

My eyes drifted to the mindless drone of the television. "So you are saying I should be one of the people guessing?"

She knew my statement was an olive branch wrapped in sarcasm and, after a sigh, took it.

"Can you put some pants on at least? You are not exactly leaving anything to the imagination right now," she said with a thin smile and diverted eyes.

We became lighthearted once again, but it felt fragile, tentative, like she was just waiting for her moment to pounce. That moment came with the next commercial.

"Ben…" she started, turning to face me. She went so far as to take my hands in hers as she peered closely at me. "What is it that you want out of life? Like, you never really seemed to want kids. Fair enough, I wouldn't want to bring any into this world either. You barely have any interest in connecting with people on a personal level anymore; so, dating and marriage seem to be out. You hated your job. You see the movement for reform as a big inconvenience and my desire to involve myself seems like a grand joke to you, even if it gives me purpose. So, what the hell is it that would make you happy?"

I didn't say anything and she shook her head in response.

"You did used to be happy. You remember

that, don't you? You used to have dreams and ambitions. Shit, you even used to put pants on without me having to strong arm you into them. It took what, like, one bad job and a breakup, and you just decided that trying was pointless?"

"An abusive boss. A terrible breakup. And dying."

"No. No. No. No." She said, swiping her hand through the air, slashing my argument out of the sky. "You don't get to use getting killed as an excuse. You were a jaded shell of a person well before that happened."

I looked at the television. "Yeah. I was." I admitted quietly. I drew in a long inhale and straightened. I'd been a coward then, too. Dying hadn't brought that trait out in me, it had only highlighted my fear. I drew in a long breath through my nose. "You said Rhapsody was asking about me?"

Kea's eyebrow popped up, intrigued by even a spark of interest in me. "She told me to bring you by the bar again." She glanced at the window and the rain falling outside. "I figured tonight, with the cold, wouldn't be the best time to drag you outside."

I shook my head and stood. "It's fine. I'll go put some pants on."

With a look of confusion, Kea stared up at me. "Wait, is this actually happening right now?"

"You can stay here. I was just going to see if she was on shift tonight, then come back."

"Come back… With her number and a date scheduled?"

I shrugged.

Kea jumped to her feet. "Oh, I am coming with. If only to make sure you don't chicken out when you get there."

"Thanks for the vote of confidence." I scooped up a pair of jeans from the floor and sniffed a discarded shirt. Passable. Barely worn and nice enough. Nice enough meaning it was a mostly fitted V-neck rather than my usual ratty t-shirt with holes from who knows how many years ago.

Kea looked me over with an appraiser's eye. "When you start inspiring confidence, I will be more willing to vote for it."

I smiled, clapping her on the shoulder. "Fair enough." I grabbed my jacket and pushed the mild ache in my joints to the back of my mind.

6

"Why, if it isn't Bennet Smith," Rhapsody said when I sidled up to the bar.

"You know my name?" For some misplaced reason that triggered alarm bells in my brain. My desire to go completely and utterly unnoticed lit up like a downtown skyscraper. I pushed that aside and forced a smile.

"I mean, you are a regular here. Or you used to be." She glanced over my shoulder, then smiled as she returned her eyes to me. "But it was Kea who told me."

"Ah, yes." That would explain it. My alarms calmed.

"So, what can I get for you, Bennet?"

"Ben. And… maybe just your number?"

She grinned. "And what would you need my number for?"

"To ask you on a date." I was astonished by my own smoothness. My ease in asking. The suave nature oozing off me. I set my hand down on a coaster and slipped, jarring me out of my blossoming conceitedness. I caught myself quickly, my hands going to my pockets instead, ego dinged.

Her smile didn't fade. Beaming and beautiful, a perfect array of teeth with one canted ever so slightly for an endearing effect. The freckles dusting her dark skin, captivating under gold-flecked eyes.

I felt instantly foolish in my attempt. This was it. I had burned my own drinking hole. I wouldn't be able to bring myself to enter this establishment again. I wrestled back the rising panic and fought my smile back onto my face. I had been out of the game far too long.

"Why don't you just ask me out and we will see about numbers after?"

"Oh, well, yes. I suppose that would work too. Would you be open to going out with me?"

"Of course, Ben. I am here today and tomorrow until close, but maybe Thursday?"

"Thursday. Yes. I am free."

"Perfect." She smiled again and grabbed a napkin and a pen. She scribbled something on the napkin, then handed it to me. "See you there, Ben."

A time. A place. "See you there, Rhapsody."

"Rap." She patted my hand, cast a wink over my shoulder at where Kea no doubt waited, then moved on down the bar.

I tucked the napkin into my jacket pocket and turned to find Kea not so discretely watching as she chatted with the bouncer.

She dismissed herself from the conversation and grabbed my arm excitedly. "You finally did it. Look at you! All grown up." She gave me a little shake. "Now, as long as we are on this journey of self-improvement, let's go get you some job applications."

"Kea…"

She ignored me, hauling me back toward the door. My eyes caught on a white stenciled tag in the corner of the community board. A hand clutching a grenade.

I frowned inwardly as Kea tugged me along behind her. I had seen that tag before and with increasing frequency.

7

I considered my bowl of noodles, thinking back on the date two nights earlier. The date had gone well, at least from my perspective. Slow to start, but Rap's constant warmth had pushed us into conversation quickly until it had flowed naturally. We had dinner before extending our outing to drinks, each of us only nursing our glasses as an excuse to continue chatting. Then I had walked her home, kissed her chastely, and did not press for more, even though I could see the welcome in her eyes.

Had I made the wrong move in going home after that? Should I have gone up to her apartment with her? We hadn't planned another evening out yet, but we had been in near constant communication. Her night shifts made finding a time difficult, and I had finally given in to Kea's constant pestering for me to get a job. I had even spent the morning working as a barista in an upper tier coffee shop, loving the hefty tips left by the caffeine starved patrons. To celebrate those fat tips, I decided to spend them on lunch in the still nice, but not as nice part of town. Somewhere I could stretch my newly acquired money a little further, but not have to worry about what type of meat was actually in my soup.

Venturing out was less the fretful chore it had been only days before. The fear of being recognized, of being nabbed by shades, or caught in a gunfight hadn't even crossed my mind. Instead, I thought of Rap. Her smile. The easy conversation and lingering brushes of fingers.

The high-rise mezzanine was crowded with folks coming and going between buildings. The bustle was strangely nice. I thought I had grown fond of the quiet being tucked away in my apartment, but with the contrast, it now felt more like I had grown lonely and bored.

My pocket buzzed and I unlocked my phone to find a message from Rap.

Rap: *I'm off Tues and Thurs this week. Let's start with one and maybe I'll give you the other.*

The corner of my mouth pulled up and I swallowed another bite of food. I stared at my phone where it sat beside my bowl trying to channel Kea into some charming response.

My attempt at manifesting wit fell flat.

Me: *Meet at Krimo Lake? The red pavilion.*
Rap: *Perf. See you there.*

I couldn't fathom why Rap had any interest in me. She didn't say it outright, but I knew that she and Kea ran in similar circles. That while I didn't have a revolutionary bone in my body, she was filled with them. Her last boyfriend had been a firebrand, waving every revolutionary flag he could find. She was sure to lose interest the moment she realized what a coward I was. But, for the moment, I could live in my little fantasy where Rhapsody Bryant wanted to go out with me on Tuesday.

I smiled at my beef noodles, not caring if others thought I was a complete doofus.

Everybody on the mezzanine stopped when the explosion rang out. We looked about, sharing furtive glances of uncertainty, but the blast had sounded far enough away. When the building didn't shudder, people returned to their business as though no concerning sound had just occurred. I was among them, turning back to my meal without a care for the muffled cry of sirens below. The small magics in the safety systems around the city would keep the fire from spreading from whatever misfortune had caused the blast. No need to fall into a panic.

The crack of gunshots stilled everybody once again. All ears canted to determine if the noise was approaching. If we should be concerned or if the fighting was contained to the streets below.

This time I frowned while everybody else returned to their business, content with the separation between us and the conflict. The explosion could have been anything. Some malfunction at a plant. A gas leak. Some mundane disaster. An explosion followed by a gunfight, though? That had my heckles up.

My mind instantly went to Kea. Those meetings she frequented. The types of stories she chased. The undercurrent of violence among the vocal minority of protesters.

I finished off my meal in two large bites, then stood. Dialing Kea, I let my feet guide me before my brain had time to process what I was doing.

"Ben?" She asked, confused by the interruption to her day.

"Where are you?" I didn't hear gunfire on her end of the connection at least.

"Well, I do have a job. So I am sitting here working it."

"On a Saturday?"

"Don't remind me," she groused. "But a deadline is a deadline and this story isn't going to write itself. Why do you ask?"

"Just making sure."

"Making sure? Is that gunfire in the background? Where are you?" Her voice peaked with concern.

"Putting distance between me and that sound. I'm headed for home."

"'Kay… Stay safe. I'll be over tonight."

It was a lie that I was putting distance between me and the gunfire. I was inexplicably walking closer to the sound.

I don't know why I went down there. Why I thought a trip down memory lane would be a good idea. A quick stop at the street of unhealed trauma. Still, I couldn't help my morbid sense of curiosity. That's what had to be driving my feet down into the killing grounds. It couldn't be any desire to help the wounded. It wasn't like there was anything I could do.

Barely employable. Not much of a catch. I definitely wasn't a hero.

Still, I descended to the streets where I had heard the gunfire. People ran in every direction except the way I was walking. The streets emptied, the fighting moving off. It was unmistakable at this point. Another massacre in the misguided attempt to quell uprising. Strike enough fear into those who were content with the status quo and you radicalize them. Everything the state was doing with its increasing oppression would only work against them in the end.

The state was just as scared as the people, though. And from the looks of it, the officers with their guns were even more terrified. The bodies in the street were those of protesters, but also of families. The majority of the bodies bore bullet wounds in their backs. They had been running. Fleeing. Just as scared of the explosion as the officers had been. They had been gunned down.

The city had barely made it a week before committing another atrocity.

I could hear the despondent mewling of the wounded, dying where they lay. Had I sounded like that? Taken down with a bullet to the hip, wallowing on the ground, just waiting for the pain to end.

I shouldn't be here. Shouldn't be on the streets with the cacophony of a gunfight not too far away. The roar of sirens as fire crews battled the flames raging from the exploded building. Even if the emergency systems could keep the fire from threatening the neighboring high-rises, the struck building was still in danger. I watched fire crews throw suppressors into the ground floor of the building down the road, letting the small magics try to calm the raging inferno within. I saw the authorities take off in pursuit of groups of runners attempting to scatter to the winds. At least with all the distractions, the officers had moved away from this point.

I edged off the main avenue, tugged along as if by some unseen rope. Even if I had run toward the gunfight, I still had the sense to try to get to some semblance of cover.

On this street, nobody moved. Only I had

ventured down. Only I was stupid enough to put myself in such danger for the sake of my morbid curiosity. What had been the site of a farmer's market was now a site of death and destruction. Tents and crafts tables still lined the streets, abandoned in the chaos. Only blood and bodies lay between the stalls.

Maybe Kea had finally started wearing off on me. Or the constant pressure of her subtle disappointment. Maybe I was driven by some desire to impress Rap. Maybe I was just tired of being useless.

But useless was exactly what I was when I crouched beside the dying woman. Her soft groans seemed an automatic response rather than any real attempt at life. Her eyes were closed, body torn apart by bullets. Laid out beside her was a man too still for life. In her rag-doll arms, a girl lay, eyes open with a shock of pain. Dead. Even with her mother's attempt at sheltering her with her body. The bullets had penetrated both small frames.

I gently removed the daughter from the mother's arms, trying to work the dying woman into a more comfortable position for her final rest. I wasn't a doctor, and even if I was, I was certain there was nothing I could do for this woman. Would she even want the help anyway, with her family dead beside her?

I closed the girl's eyes and set her beside her mother. Then I sat, holding the woman's hand in some fool's attempt at providing comfort. I didn't hear the gunfire anymore. Not because the fighting had stopped. It had only intensified, in fact. I couldn't see past the blood. The girl's still chest. The emptiness of this slaughter. My eyes found the scatter of color where the bouquet the man had been holding had been crushed under his falling body. The reusable bag filled with vegetables. A family's visit to the farmer's market and this is what befell them?

I held the woman's limp hand until her rasping breath ceased. I sat longer still, ignoring the ache in my bones and the atrophy of my muscles with the stillness.

Steadily, I set the woman's hand down. But I didn't straighten. Something felt not quite right. Unfinished. Like I shouldn't leave just yet. I looked at the man's body, still as it had been when I found them. My eyes fell to the girl. Young, so young. And now dead.

I frowned, not knowing what it was that kept me where I sat. There was something, though. Something that told me to wait just a moment longer.

The gasping rattle of a breath drawn through a mire startled me to my feet. My legs protested the sudden movement and my muscles sang out. The gasp turned to a lung hacking fit of coughs. The girl rolled from her back to her side, trembling, coughing, spitting out gobs of blood as her lungs reclaimed the space for breath. She spasmed violently, then stilled again, but this time I could see that her breath had returned.

And with that, she had started her second life.

I stood staring, dumb and immobile.

The girl had returned to life. I looked at her mother and father; hopeful, desperate. Neither body stirred. That feeling that had kept me rooted moments before was gone. Only desperation kept me where I was. I was a deer caught in the headlights. Everything in me told me to run for it. I couldn't do anything for this girl. Everything in me told me to scoop her up and take her with me. I knew I couldn't leave her alone. Just a child, already dead and returned once. Her family gone. Before I knew exactly what I was doing, I was kneeling beside the girl, gently working my arms under her and lifting her from the cold pavement.

The sounds of the gunfight suddenly returned to me and I glanced back toward the ongoing struggle. I needed to get off the streets. To get home. To get this girl home.

8

I left the girl to rest, remembering how painful the return could be. Her physical wounds were healed, but the scars would linger beneath the surface. The trauma. The pain of death remembered. She would need time. Not just to regain her energy, but to regain her strength.

Staring at her while she slept wasn't going to be of any help. So I set a blanket over her, got myself cleaned up, and made myself useful.

Kea was right. I knew she was. It wasn't fair of me to leave my mess in the hallways. If the landlord wasn't going to put in the work to keep our living space nice, I may as well.

I grabbed a trash bag and some gloves and set in on the hallways. Today I would collect the trash hiding in the corners and evict the dust bunnies. Tomorrow maybe the burned out lightbulbs so I could see what the extent of the damage we were dealing with was.

I set about the task with a single-mindedness, seeking distraction. I didn't notice Farah watching me shuffle by before ducking into her apartment to grab a rag for the handrails. I didn't notice Griffin milling about with a broom.

We had never really talked, keeping our communications to the obligatory head bob as we passed in the halls. That made the experience easier as we all worked in silence. Griffin disappeared with the broom and reemerged with a box of lightbulbs. Some old, some new, but all in better condition than the spent bulbs overhead. I chucked my bag of trash into the back-alley dumpster and helped Griffin manage the box of bulbs. Still without more than a few grunts serving as communication. We had all grown accustomed to keeping our heads down.

Maybe that was another thing Kea was right about. Keeping quiet, keeping our eyes fixed on the ground, kept us isolated, kept us stuck in the status quo.

I looked down the hall at where Farah worked, one of her small children now scrubbing the wall beside her. I glanced at Griffin as he carefully screwed in another bulb. I considered saying something, some inane words that would at least breach the silence we were so used to.

Whatever empty nonsense I wanted to put out into the world fizzled in my throat. We had already made progress today. Why push it?

9

I wasn't surprised to hear a knock announcing Kea's arrival. I glanced up from the egg scramble I was cooking to confirm it was her walking into my apartment.

Kea looked around as she strolled in. "You finally complain to the landlord? The place looks… Well, not nice, but less shit? Is that how you would describe it?"

I chuckled and rolled my eyes. "Thanks. I worked really hard on it."

"You? You cleaned up the building?"

I shrugged. "You were right. It's not fair of me to leave my mess in the communal spaces. And if I don't clean it up, nobody else will."

She narrowed her eyes at me. "Who are you, and what did you do with Ben? You know? Ben. The little shit who doesn't do anything for anybody if there's no payday involved." She eyed me with suspicion, glancing down at my frying pan with a hint of surprise. "I didn't know your stove still even worked. All I ever see you eat are boxes of cereal and packaged sandwiches."

"I thought you would be happy to see me

put in a little effort." To be fair, I too had been surprised when the old flame cooktop had managed to ignite.

She smiled and set a hand on my shoulder. "I am. I'm just confused. What brought this on? Is Rap coming over? Or... Wait. Are you actually wearing pants?"

I winced. "Yeah. Terrible as it is. I thought it was prudent, considering..." I nodded toward the girl sleeping on the couch.

She frowned, then her eyes snapped wide. "Is that a child? Who's child is that?"

I shook my head, turning off the flame on the stove, feeling a little tug in my fingertips as the small magic sputtered and died. I hadn't noticed the sensation before dying and I had never used the stove after. I dismissed the thought and wiped my hands on the dish towel over my shoulder.

"I don't know. I probably should have grabbed their wallets. I didn't think rolling their bodies was the sensitive thing to do. But... I don't know who she is..." I was looking past the girl on the couch, my gaze distant, fixed in blood. I blinked the memory clear. "She was dead." I looked at Kea. "Then she wasn't."

Kea looked from the girl to me, sorrow in her eyes. "Shit." She said, voice quiet. "The gunfire? Her parents?"

"I think they were the ones with her. They certainly looked like her folks. I don't know.

And she has barely woken up except to cough up more blood and bullets." Her body would be rejecting all foreign objects hard and fast right now, repairing the damage done with alarming haste before settling back into an approximation of life and its slow, inelegant healing processes.

Kea swallowed. "What are you going to do with her?"

"I don't know." I shook my head. "I think it will take her a while to really wake up. The damage was pretty bad and she's so young." It had taken my tortured body over a week to have enough energy to stand again after my death. But it had also taken whatever wild magic pieced me back together hours to revive me, still hanging from my noose. I swallowed, my throat dry at the memory. "Maybe she has some family, but I can't bring her to the authorities. Especially not like this. They will know she died once."

My mind was spinning. While on the record Second Lifes were not discriminated against, it wasn't something many who had died wanted anybody else to know about, especially the state. There were rumors that Second Life drifters went missing in the night, never to be seen again. It wouldn't surprise me to find out that the loners had found themselves strapped down to a table in some lab where they could be studied mercilessly. Nobody understood why we started coming back to life. But, oh, if they could figure it out.

I spooned the eggs onto a plate, banishing yet another dark thought.

"I figured she would need the protein."

Kea looked at the eggs, then at me. Her brow seemed fixed in its furrow. "You can't just take a kid in, Ben. You are not exactly… you know…"

I scoffed. "Thanks again for yet another vote of confidence. I don't intend to keep her. But I couldn't leave her there. And I couldn't think what else to do." I swallowed. "I thought maybe you could help me figure that out."

"I don't know anything about kids, man."

"I know. I know. I'll ask Em. Maybe she knows the right processes." I hadn't talked to my sister since my death, but I also hadn't talked to her much before, so she couldn't really hold the recent silence against me. I hoped.

"You can't put this on Emily," Kea said, shaking her head. "That's not fair to her."

"You are only telling me no, Kea. I'm not hearing any solutions here. Besides, this gives me something to talk to Emily about. Maybe smooth things over with us."

"A random Second Life kid being dropped in her lap is not a means to smoothing anything over with your sister." Her mouth pinched in a way I knew all too well, and she looked off to the side. She had stopped herself from saying something.

"What was that?"

"Nothing. Just… You don't need an excuse to talk to your sister. One. And two, she's not mad at you." The pinched lips resolved. "She's giving you space."

"Space? Wait. You told her?"

Kea scoffed. "She saw the news broadcast. You think your own sister didn't recognize you? After you came back, you didn't tell her, so I did. I couldn't just leave her in her grief waiting for you to get your head out of your ass enough to realize you are not the only person in the world who was affected by your death." She cut herself off, her chin pulling toward her chest as though she were being reined in, and she bit her lip. She looked thoroughly rebuked, but everything she had said was valid.

I looked down. "I should have called her. It shouldn't have been on you to tell her. I'm sorry."

She shook her head, but didn't say anything.

I looked at the girl still sleeping on the couch. She had started to stir at the sudden outburst and would maybe open her eyes soon. "I don't know what I'm doing. I don't know what I am going to do. I need help."

"Call your sister." She grabbed the plate and a fork and brought both to the coffee table to wait for the girl to finish waking up. "But first. I think we need to talk to her," she said with a nod toward the girl.

Kea was right, of course. I couldn't be making any decisions for the girl without giving her a say in what to do with her second life. Nobody had to know she had even been on that street. Nobody had to know she had died. I had needed Kea's calm confidence to give me a breath to think.

I sat on the coffee table in front of the girl as her eyes flitted open. Exhausted black orbs looked back at me. Weary, confused, then wide with shock and fear. She sat up, throwing the blanket covering her to the side, and looked around hurriedly.

"It's okay. You are safe now," I said. I could see in her eyes that she remembered her death. I could read it in the way her hands grasped at where her body had been shredded by bullets. She didn't say anything, and that drove a spike of fear into my chest. The silence was a terror I hadn't been prepared for. A scream. A wail. Blubbering sobs. Anything. But there was nothing. Her grasping fingers loosened and fell to her lap, and her startled eyes slackened with acceptance. She released a small puff of breath and that was it.

My eyes flicked to Kea, only to receive a shrug in answer.

The girl's gaze slackened, and a detached

look overtook her. She had looked smaller when she had been unconscious and curled up. Now that she was up, she looked older. Maybe it was just her hollow gaze or empty expression. Maybe it was the realization of her own death that had aged her so swiftly. "I'm supposed to be dead." Young as she was, her voice was firm and certain in that statement. Death had a way. Especially with children. Her eyes drifted to the plate of eggs I held in offering.

She didn't move to take the plate, so I set it awkwardly in her lap, pressing the fork against her hand until she realized what I wanted and gripped it. Her body needed the sustenance.

"Do you know where your home is?" Maybe that was a stupid question. What would she have at home without her parents? I was always uncomfortable with children. They were always feral things to me, but this girl had lost everything in one moment. I could at least make an effort. I revised myself. "Do you have somewhere you can go?"

She didn't answer, instead turning her attention to the eggs. She ate them with determination. Her body needed fuel to replenish what had been lost, not that it ever truly could.

10

Kea had dipped out hours before, but I wasn't surprised when she showed up at my door again later that evening. It was late. The sky was dark, and the girl was deeply asleep once again.

"I went out to the spot… You know… Where she…" Kea said in hushed tones, trying to avoid any contentious words in case the girl could hear us. I knew how deeply she slept though. She shouldn't be interrupting any time soon. Kea pulled out her phone, showing me a set of photos. A couple of identification cards. "Were these them?"

I squinted at the pictures and nodded. The girl's parents looked younger in their photos but there was no mistaking their faces. I tried not to notice the charcoal gray jacket framing the ID cards in the background of each photo. The girl's father's back.

"I thought maybe it would be helpful if you had their names and her address. But I didn't feel right swiping their wallets. The baggers might need their IDs and all." She was rambling in a way that was entirely unlike Kea. "There were a lot of bodies. I had to sort through a little, based on the description you gave. The streets were calm, but the baggers didn't seem like they were in any hurry to gather up the remains." She caught herself in her ramble and shook herself to recenter. She handed me a wad of cash. "I did take this, though. They don't exactly need it. It's only enough for maybe a nice meal. You'll need to feed her. I remember how ravenous you got." Her eyes drifted toward the empty couch. "She's still here, isn't she?"

I nodded. "I gave her my bed. I figured it's the least I can do. And I'm used to falling asleep on the couch anyway." I straightened out the paper bills and tucked them into my wallet. If Kea hadn't taken the money, some other grifter rolling bodies would have. Maybe I would have balked at the idea of picking the pockets of the dead in the past, but now, if I had been in the right frame of mind when I had found the girl, I knew I would have done the same.

Kea washed her hands then wandered to the lounger where she sank into its worn cushions. She pulled the lever that released the footrest and kicked up her feet.

I sank into the couch across from her, the two of us sharing a heavy sigh. We sat in silence for a long time, each of us staring off into our own private abyss. I tossed her a blanket, realizing she had no intention of leaving that night, then sprawled out on the couch and shut my eyes.

11

We didn't leave my apartment all Sunday. The girl spent the day in bed, only waking up to eat and use the bathroom. She didn't say a word as she moved between the two rooms and only mumbled what sounded like 'thanks' when I presented her with another plate. I spent the day alternating between the couch and the stove, where I kept the eggs cooking. I wasn't a culinary genius by any means, but the girl didn't seem to care. She diligently scarfed down each plate of eggs, her body's need for the protein overriding any disgust at eating the same dish on repeat.

On Monday, I found her curled up on the recliner. The blanket Kea had left neatly folded on it that morning tucked around her as she flipped through channels. She lingered on reruns of long since ended game shows and back-to-back infomercials.

When I stirred, she glanced at me before her eyes flicked to the stove.

"You got it, Kid. We will have to run out and get some groceries if you keep this up, though."

She gave me a small nod before returning to her mindless channel surfing.

***

We caught Emily supervising her students during recess. The school was one of those overcrowded, underfunded public messes, but Emily always seemed to enjoy the work. The idea of spending an entire day trying to force children to learn sounded like a nightmare to me, but Emily had been doing it for years.

Diligent of her charges as ever, Emily's eyes darted to me as soon as she spotted strangers on the approach. Her expression contorted with surprise, then hardened and she stormed over to the fence.

I braced for her assault, before remembering I had ambushed her at work for a reason. It was the one place she wouldn't let her tirade loose.

"This isn't fair, Ben," she said through clenched teeth.

I nodded. "I know. But. I need you."

"Need me for what?"

"Need you to, sort of, watch her," I said, grimacing as I fished the girl out from behind me. "Just for a little bit. I have to run out and grab some things."

"What? No. Bennet. This isn't some daycare. You can't just leave random kids here."

"Nobody will notice one more kid in your class. She looks like she's about the same size as the other ones. She'll blend right in." I shrugged then hefted the girl over the fence with a grunt, seeing that her feet were squarely on the ground before releasing her shoulders. "Hey, have fun with the other kids. Be nice. I'll be back in a couple hours," I said to the girl, patting her on the back.

She just stared at me doe eyed but didn't argue.

Emily was a different story.

"No, Bennet. You can't just show up after… You can't…" She gave a frustrated growl, running her hand through her hair. "That's not how this works!" She tried to grab my arm before I could recall it back over the fence, but when the girl took off to join the other kids, she sighed and rolled her eyes. "One of the kids didn't show up today anyway," she groused, resigned to watch this wayward mystery child. "What's her name at least?"

"If you can get it out of her, let me know. I've just been calling her 'kid'."

"You owe me an actual conversation after this, Bennet."

I nodded my agreement to those terms. "I'll be back by the end of the school day. I promise. I just have to run some errands real quick." I stuffed my hands into my pockets, feeling the sheet of notepaper that I had scribbled the girl's address onto. "What time does school get out, by the way?"

"Three o'clock. You better not be late."

"Three. Got it." I nodded. "Can I buy you dinner tonight?"

"I can't do dinner tonight. I am cooking at home with my kids. I wish you had called so I could have planned enough food for us all." Emily sighed and looked back toward the playground. "I'll see you at three." Her arms were crossed and her lips puckered, but she wasn't arguing, so I took my leave. I had to get across town and back in a matter of hours or face her wrath.

Two buses, a short jaunt on the cross-city train, and a final bus brought me to the family home. The house was quiet. It was all too possible that the authorities hadn't reported the deaths to their next of kin yet. It was possible there were no next of kin. It was just as likely that the bodies were still rotting on the street where they had fallen. I pushed the thought away as I circled the premise, checking the street for any looky-loo do-gooders that would report my next actions.

The residence was a small family home in a part of town that was only moderately run down. There were few single-family residences left in the city, but small pockets of holdouts remained here and there. The home owners just waiting for the next developer to come along with a blank check. Few people risked living outside the cities anymore, driving the need for housing through the roof, even as the wastes beyond the city limits went relatively untouched.

Every year, the developers continued their spread out at only a slow crawl. Few people liked the idea of living so close to the edge. There were too many ghost stories about untamed magics and gangs of murderous cannibals roving the wastes on the outskirts of the city. I wasn't sure I quite bought into all the nonsense. Still, I did live far from the edges.

This family, though, they had been rather close to the eastern limit. Seemed they weren't concerned about the creep of magic when there were so many other, more serious concerns in everyday life in Zenith.

Contrary to their name, the wastes were a tangle of untamed jungles, thick with brambles and vines. Rather than 'a wasteland', they were 'a waste of space', according to the developers who struggled to penetrate the wilds. It was a costly venture hacking through jungle so dense that their machinery was often overtaken and swallowed whole by vines, or rusted and decayed by the wild magics in the winds. If the stories were to be believed, the wastes hadn't always been so aggressive. The scientists who fought to tame and harness the wild magics claimed they had no idea why the danger of the wastes had amped up in recent years. But looking at the equally aggressive expansion of megacities, I had my suspicions.

From the back porch, I could see the rising waves of green where treetops peeked over rooftops. The divide where wild magics resumed their dominance beyond Zenith's bounds.

A warm wind blew in from the wastes, making me shudder. Maybe it made sense why people on the edge ventured in to the center. The very air near the edge felt thicker, more unstable. Wild magic was a random beast, with no rhyme or reason. I didn't remember the edge feeling so muggy during my last visit, but that had also been at least fifteen years ago.

I smashed the backdoor window and waited for an alarm. When none sounded, I pressed into the home. I stalked through the space silently, wary of an attack that wasn't likely to come.

"Why the hell were you so deep in the city yesterday?" I muttered to myself as I looked over the family photos. They had so much here. To have come into the city had been foolish. It had cost them their lives. They had been paying a nice part of the city a visit. They must have assumed nothing bad could happen. They hadn't seen how quickly even the nice parts of town could go bad these days. Tension was running high everywhere and idiots with guns could be anywhere. At least near the edges, all they had to worry about were strange winds and creeping vines.

I shuffled through their belongings, trying to figure anything out about the family, gathering up all the information I could before finding the girl's room. I grabbed the bookbag that was hanging from a peg by her door and stuffed it full of the girl's clothes without discerning what I was grabbing. I didn't know which shirts were her favorites, which pants she hated wearing. All I knew was that she needed clothing and these would hopefully fit her. She couldn't keep wandering through town in one of my shirts tied and tucked to keep the bagginess at bay and a pair of my shorts with a belt strapped tight at the waist. With a glance at her bed, I decided to snatch up the stuffed cat that lay tucked in, crushing it into the bag with the clothes.

I made one last pass through the house, popping a few of the pictures out of their frames and sliding them into the bag before it was time to go. Even if she didn't want the memories now, maybe one day she would.

I made it back to the school just in time to see Emily walking out the front doors, releasing her charges back to their waiting parents. The girl flitted around between several children, not saying much but with a smile on her face as they all said their parting words of the day.

I could read the suspicion on my sister's face as she scanned the crowd, not really expecting to see me. I gave a small wave. Enough to draw her attention and loosen a sigh that looked like it wavered between relief and uncertainty. I jogged up the steps to her, waiting while she exchanged a few words with a colleague or a parent. I couldn't tell the difference.

Emily turned toward me. "Wasn't sure you were actually coming back."

"Didn't even cross my mind not to."

"She told me her name is Sara. But it seems like she was just making it up."

After my visit to her home, I knew the name was a lie, but if she wanted to leave her past life behind, that was her prerogative. "If it's what she wants to be called, it's better than 'kid,' I guess."

Emily looked at Sara, her voice dropping to a whisper. "Is she…"

"A Second Life? Yeah."

"How did you find her?"

"She was visiting the Midtown Farmer's Market with her family. I happened to be in the area and I guess like calls to like."

Emily grimaced, aware of the news reports that had finally broken on the gunfight, fabricated as they may be.

"It was bad luck for everybody caught up in it," I said quietly. "Thanks for watching her."

"Did you take care of what you needed?"

I held up the child's backpack loaded with her clothing and the well-loved stuffed animal. "Got a few of her things. We'll see if she will even look at them. She seems intent on forgetting her life."

With a deep set frown, Emily watched the girl play with the stragglers still waiting for pickup. "I can't even begin to imagine the trauma of death." Her eyes turned to me. "I didn't expect to ever see you play dad."

I cringed at the thought. "Just... Looking after her. The way I died and the way she did are two very different things but, us Second Lifes gotta stick together. The world is a hell of a place."

Emily nodded and said quietly, "It is. But what are you doing to change it?"

I cast her a sideways look while she cast one right back at me. "You've been chatting with Kea too much."

She shook her head. "Kea doesn't hold the monopoly on feelings of discontent."

I sniffed. "Fair point." I clicked my tongue. "I'm not doing much, but maybe a little bit of good." My eyes were fixed on the girl. "At least, I hope I am doing enough that I am not doing any harm." I beckoned to the girl. "You ready to go, Sara?" I asked, pointedly using her chosen name.

For a moment she hesitated on the lie, then

beamed with acceptance of the new identity and nodded. As she made her way over, Emily's eyes followed her.

"If it ever gets to be too much for you, you'll call me, right?" She asked, not looking at me.

"You really doubt my ability that much?"

"A parent is just nothing I ever expected you to be."

I was about to argue that I wasn't a parent, then felt the sinking pit of realization that there was every potential that was exactly what I was about to become if I couldn't find the girl's family. Sara darted up to me expectantly, and it took me a moment to snap back to myself enough to sink to a crouch for the kid to clamor onto my back.

I held the backpack up where Sara could grab it, uncertain if the girl's determined avoidance of her past extended to objects. I felt her hesitate, then grab the bag, and while I was careful to support her, she slung it onto her back obligingly.

I fished a granola bar from my pocket and held it up to her. "I'm guessing you're hungry. No allergies I should know about, right?"

Sara shook her head and snatched the bar.

"Sorry if it's a little warm…"

She didn't seem to mind as she tore open the bar and chewed loudly beside my ear.

"You are coming over tomorrow," Emily said decisively.

"Can't tomorrow. I have a date."

"A date? Really?" She almost looked impressed. "Well, then, Sara, you will come over tomorrow, right?" The girl nodded tentatively. Emily smiled warming, winning the girl to her side. "You can stay the night if you want. Then I can bring you to school with me."

"I thought that's not how that worked," I pointed out.

"The school is so overcrowded. What's one more? Every child is owed an education." She looked at Sara, waiting for her agreement. She finished chewing, her arms tightening around my shoulders, but she nodded once again. "Then it's settled." My sister looked back to me. "Bring her here tomorrow, then meet us here at three on Wednesday. You and I are going to talk." She left no room for argument and I nodded. "I'm cooking. I don't want to find out what you think passes for food." She looked at Sara. "The invitation is for both of you."

"Thanks for looking after her," I said.

Emily looked like she wanted to say something more, but only nodded.

***

My apartment complex didn't look as dingy when we got back. Seemed the bug for cleaning had caught. Even the oldest and grouchiest of the neighbors was out sweeping the front step rather than just sitting there brooding with a phantom cigarette between her fingers. Tabacco had gone the way of the dodo years before. A blight many believed was caused by feral wild magics breaching our border protections ravaged the farms. If that was the case, maybe the wild magics were trying to look after our health and wellbeing. I couldn't imagine why. We certainly didn't deserve it.

Since leaving the school, we hadn't said a single word after my initial attempt at small talk fell flat.

Sara tossed the backpack in the corner and that's where it would sit for several days. Only the cat disappeared. I later found it locked tightly in her arms while she slept.

12

I wasn't surprised when Sara slept through me getting ready and leaving for work the next morning. Nor was I surprised to find her still sleeping when I returned that afternoon, the breakfast I had left for her in the fridge untouched. She was still recovering and the day of school had likely stretched her past her limit. I was considering canceling on Emily and Rap when she finally emerged from my room, rubbing her eyes. Her bleary gaze drifted from me to the kitchen and I dutifully stood to warm up some food for her.

"Still want to go to Emily's tonight?" I asked while she sat at the table watching me at the stove.

She nodded, sleep still thick but abating.

I set her plate in front of her and she started shoveling the food into her mouth as if she hadn't eaten in weeks. There was no point reminding her to slow down. She needed the fuel.

"And you can do another day of school tomorrow? I can always cancel my date, or swing by after to pick you up." For once, I wasn't looking for an excuse to get out of a social engagement.

She looked up from her food and shook her head.

"Alright. If you are sure. Then when you are done eating, we will head over."

Sara ignored the backpack and instead found a simple drawstring bag, shoving her toothbrush and cat into it before walking toward the door. When we got down to the street, her fingers slid into my hand and held tight.

I looked down at her. There was a nervousness in the way her eyes darted here and there. I recognized a similar fear to the one I had felt for so long. I needed to push that back now. I gave her hand a silent squeeze and she seemed to relax.

Why she trusted me, I couldn't understand, but her hand didn't leave mine the entire way to Emily's apartment.

My sister's building was much nicer than mine. Newer. Taller. Cleaner. And it sported a green space between the other buildings in the complex where several families were out enjoying the day. Sara eyed the playground and the children clamoring over the structure.

"Nicer than mine, isn't it? I should make a point of coming by more often. We used to do dinner all the time years ago." I led her toward the building. "I haven't been over since... You know…"

This time it was Sara who gave my hand a comforting squeeze, and I chuckled, throwing a reassuring smile her way.

I felt a hum around me as the elevator rose. One that I had only started to take notice of after I had died. It was similar to the one that came from my phone and the harnessed magics of the vehicles on the streets. It was something I had never really felt until it had been tearing through me as my second life took hold. Now it was unmistakable and everywhere. For once, I savored the fact that my building's lift had never been fixed. Every step on my climb home was a different sort of agony while encumbered by grocery bags, but at least the climb didn't bring back memories of a rope burning the soft flesh of my neck.

Sara's hand twitched in mine, and I tightened my grip. Weeks into my second life I had stopped constantly noticing the tug of small magics in the world around me, but watching Sara's eyes widen and dart around reminded me how distracting the new sensation had been initially. Especially around newer technologies.

At Emily's door, I crouched, meeting Sara's eye. "I'm not trying to dump you. I can always come pick you up if you need. Just have Emily call me."

She gave a half smile before giving me a

hug. "Have fun," she whispered her quiet blessing in my ear.

Her voice was a small, musical thing.

"She will be alright, Ben," Emily assured me, looking down at us.

"I know she will." I straightened. Emily waved Sara into her apartment with a smiled. "She's going to eat more than you expect. And sleep hard. If you need anything—"

"Ben..."

I swallowed. "Yes. I know. You are a great mom. I should stop worrying."

"Exactly. Go enjoy your date. I don't imagine you have been out on many recently." She pulled me into a hug. "Three tomorrow at the school. You will tell me how tonight went."

There was no way my big sister was going to let me off the hook so easily.

"I'm sorry it was Kea who told you. I should have called."

Emily shook her head, still holding me tight. "I've had a lot of time to be angry at you, Ben. But at the end of the day, I'm just happy you are alive." She held me at arm's length, looking me over. "Whatever the circumstances, I am glad to have you back in my life. Now go, before you are late."

13

The date had gone so well. Somehow I had managed to be charming, and even in my stumbles, Rap still managed to laugh graciously and hold my arm. There was something so natural about the way we clicked.

I took her hand, savoring the warmth of her palm against mine and the smile on her lips as we strolled through Besgrow Park. The sun was setting and it would be smart to head indoors, but I didn't want the night to end just yet. So, I listened to her talk about this and that as we meandered through the city as neon replaced sunlight.

I only realized she had been guiding us when we came to a stop in front of a familiar high-rise condominium. Rap leaned back from me, looking up and back at the building, relying on my hands holding her to keep her from falling. She smiled and righted herself.

"This is mine," she said, dropping one of my hands and taking a step back.

That was that. We had reached the end once again. I nodded, feeling a small pit waver in my stomach.

She dropped my other hand to dig in her purse, drawing out a metal keycard. Fancier than the old-style turnkeys in my ramshackle of a building. She backed toward the looming doors of her building, eyes flicking to my feet as if to see if I would follow. I could see her tongue playing behind her teeth with her lips slightly parted. She gave me a coy look and a wink, then turned to bound up the steps of her building. I watched her curls bounce away before she turned to look back at me.

"Well, hurry up, now. Can't just hold the door open for you all night. The night guard might get upset."

I didn't need to be prompted twice. I darted up the steps before reminding myself to play casual. I was anything but. But Rhapsody Bryant had just invited me up to her unit.

She beeped us in and I smiled as I held the door for her.

The guard eyed us with a bored look before returning his attention to the sporting event playing out on the screen beside him. Rap entwined her fingers with mine and led me to the lifts. Whatever small magics lay trapped in the mechanisms were beyond me, but the ride up to her floor was fast and silent. My insides were humming so loudly I was surprised I even notice the magics driving the lift. But once I did, my nerves latched on and all I could think about was the small magics sliding around me, the feel of something wild and raw so tamed. A shadow of the force that had welcomed me gracelessly back to life.

Rap's fingers tightened around my hand, drawing my attention away from the hum, and back to her. The sultry look in her eye had dampened, replaced with a question.

The lift stopped and the doors opened. With the mechanisms no longer in motion, the hum abated enough that the distraction of her fully pulled my attention back to the now. I smiled. The curiosity in her eyes remained, but she let it drop as she tugged me toward her unit.

"It's a nice building," I commented, eyeing the freshly cleaned carpets and neatly painted walls that lined the halls. It was a far cry from one of the buildings filled with the wealthy, but a guard at the door, clean carpets, and fresh paint on the walls was leagues ahead of my filthy hovel. I doubted any lightbulb was allowed to flicker long in this building.

I felt a moment of embarrassment at the realization that I could never invite her over after seeing this. But when I looked at her, I saw she had a flash of pink on her cheeks.

"It is." She agreed timidly. "My, uh, my dad didn't like my old building, so he took over a lease here and, you know," she shrugged, "I didn't want to let it go to waste." She said it with such shame that I regretted bringing it up.

"Well, just wait till you see my place," I said

with a grin in a weak attempt at lightening the mood again.

She returned the grin with a smirk. "Easy, tiger. Let's not make any assumptions about a third date. The night is still young and you might just find yourself with your foot in your mouth yet."

She tapped her keycard against the door beside her and drew me into her unit.

"I would tell you I invited you up for a nightcap, but I don't actually keep any alcohol around." She said, kicking her shoes off and drawing me further into her condo. A long corridor greeted us with doors along it leading to ensuite laundry and a freshly kept bathroom before spilling out into an elegantly furnished dining room and respectable kitchen. "What I can offer you is a bottle of sparkling water or a variety of juices."

"A variety, you say?"

"A veritable cornucopia." She flitted over to the refrigerator and opened the door to display the options as though it were a new car on one of the various game shows that flooded the nets.

"I'll take a water. Thanks," I said, trying not to look uncomfortable in the space. It wasn't the most glamorous of abodes, but it screamed of comfort. Somehow, I could tell that Rap's father hadn't sprung for something pricier for fear that his daughter might reject something too nice. But the appliances in the kitchen put mine to shame. The dining table that looked rarely used was actual wood. The ceilings were high enough to ward away any feelings of claustrophobia. And the view wasn't just of the building next door. The lifts had taken us high enough to peek over several of the surroundings buildings. The imperfections of the location felt contrived. I kept my thoughts to myself as I took the bottle Rap offered me.

"I guess I'm surprised you don't keep any alcohol on hand given you're a bartender."

"Do you have an espresso machine at home, given you are a barista?" she asked, a touch defensive. She smoothed it away quickly and took a seat on the couch, patting the cushion next to her. "Sorry. Your foot got precariously close to your mouth just now."

"I'm sorry." I fought the urge to bite my lip as I lingered in uncertainty.

She patted the cushion again and I sat.

Once I was seated, she shook her head. "I get a little touchy about it, but it's a fair enough question. Take it this way, I learned the skill of bartending from my mother." I could tell from the look in her eye that the memory was a painful one and let the matter lie.

She had folded her hands in her lap. I set mine on hers for a moment and squeezed lightly. Just enough to say I was there for her before taking my hand back.

She looked at my fingers. "You know, you are a real gentleman?" A smile flashed on her lips. "So, what was that back in the lift?"

"Just… memories…"

"Fair enough. I won't push you."

I gave her a smile then asked, "Do you feel magic? Like the hum of small magics?"

"Um…" She said in confusion, but her head cocked to the side as though she were trying to listen to something. "I can't say I have ever tried to… Where did that question come from?"

"Just… The elevator. I can't remember noticing it before, but I could swear I felt the magic in the mechanisms humming. That's what distracted me."

She shrugged. "It is an older one. It can get a little shaky from time to time — perfectly safe, just shakes a little. Maybe that's what it was." Old to her was much newer than I tended to be used to, I guessed.

She grinned suddenly, as though an idea had struck her. "I didn't exactly ask you up here to talk about elevators." Rap circled around to my front and straddled my lap. I smiled, my hands finding her hips, perfectly content to let the matter rest. To let myself pretend for a moment that I didn't feel the brief hum of magic as one of our phones received a message. I tipped my head up to her, fingers tightening on her waist, then stopped. I had Rhapsody in front of me. On top of me, even.

Why was I hesitating?

"What's wrong?" She asked, leaning down to kiss me.

I returned the kiss, trying to will away the feeling of deception creeping through my bones, but it had dug in deep. I pulled back slightly and looked up at her. "I… I don't want to go any further without telling you…"

She sat up straight, a curious look in her eyes.

"Remember how I disappeared for a few months?"

"Yeah."

I sighed, looking down as I pushed back the unwelcome memories. "I got picked up by the shades. That's why I disappeared. I spent weeks in interrogation, after spending weeks being beaten and left in the dark…" I sucked in air through my nose and looked up at her, the sad sinking feeling in her eyes palpable. "To make a long and horrible story short… I… I'm a Second Life."

"A Second Life?" She frowned. "You mean they killed you? You died and came back?"

I nodded.

She sat heavily on my legs. My fingers tensed involuntarily to support her. Her hands locked behind my neck as she looked down at me. "That's some heavy shit," she said inwardly. "Really heavy shit. Why did you tell me?"

"It seemed important. Especially since I'm… well… you know… and I didn't want you to find out after…"

She leaned down, kissing me tenderly this time. The hunger had cooled, but the fire continued to smolder. Her hands cupped my cheeks. "I'm sorry that happened to you." She swallowed, her eyes locked on mine. "It doesn't change how I feel about you. You are alive now, and that's what matters."

14

The soft chirping of my phone alarm woke me in the morning. Thankfully, Rap slept through the quiet melody. The woman rolled over and away from the sound, so all I could see of her was her mess of dark curls and the rise of her hip under the covers.

The night had been amazing, the sex even better. Leaving before she even woke up felt like a slap, but she had known I had the early shift when she invited me to stay over. I dressed as quietly as I could before slipping out of her room on silent feet. A text felt impersonal, but saying nothing felt even worse.

Me: *I'll be thinking about you all day.*

Maybe being too honest was a turnoff. Or maybe I should get out of my head and stop second guessing every little interaction. The evening had been amazing. She had invited me to stay over. I needed to stop worrying so much.

True to my word, I spent the bus ride

thinking about Rap. About our night and what I could do to make our next date special. The only thing that snapped me from my happy reprieve was the scratched sketch of a fist wrapped around a grenade on the back of the bus seat in front of me.

I frowned at the sketch, my finger tracing over the jagged lines. I had been killed for this damn revolution. So many had. And for what? What had anybody gained? An increasingly oppressive state? More twitchy fingers on anxious triggers? My hand dropped from the etching. I turned my attention out the window.

The sky was still dark, as early as it was in the morning, but the streets of Zenith were always lit. Most of the convenience stores that lined the avenues were closed and shuttered, but a handful of gaming bars and lounges beckoned to the occasional passerby.

My eyes snagged on an advertisement on one of the larger storefronts. *Bedroom blowout. Mattresses. Bed frames. Decor. All on sale. All priced to move. Make your house a home without breaking the bank.* Alongside an array of photos of extravagant bedrooms with sprawling king beds was one of a children's room. Never in a million years would I be able to afford an apartment that could host such large beds, but maybe I could make what I had work. Help Sara feel more at home as she settled into her new reality. Besides, this arrangement with the kid was only temporary until I could figure out what to do. The setup didn't have to be perfect, it just had to work for a little while.

I pulled out my phone, intending to text Kea. My finger hovered over the back button before I instead lowered my thumbs to the keypad.

Me: *Think you can help me with something over at mine before your shift tonight?*

I hit send on the message to Rap before I could second guess it, then flicked over to text Kea.

Me: *I'm going to need some help moving furniture today.*
Kea: *You owe me, Bennet.*

***

I wasn't built for hauling furniture up several flights of stairs. Maybe Kea was with all her rippling muscles, but even she seemed winded when we finally finished getting my new additions from the street up to my unit.

"You should really ask your landlord to fix your lift," Kea muttered at me, taking a breather on the couch.

I sat opposite her with a grateful sigh, wiping beads of sweat from my forehead, slicking back my messy mop of hair with the moisture. I knuckled my hip where the bullet had shattered my pelvis, working away the phantom pains.

"Usually I don't mind the exercise," I agreed, staring at the boxed bedframe. It hadn't looked as heavy at the store, but after several flights of stairs, anything could feel heavy.

I pulled out my phone under the guise of checking the time, but really I glanced at my texts.

Rap: *Only two dates in and already asking for favors?*

She had made me sweat over that for only a few moments before her follow-up had come through.

Rap: *Send me your address.*

"Things are going that good, eh?" Kea smirked at me, knowing exactly what I was looking at.

"They seem to be, yeah. She's coming by to help get things set up before Sara gets home."

"Sara?"

"She chose it. I wasn't going to argue." I shrugged.

"Fair enough. Is she opening up at all?"

Once again, I shrugged.

"Once again. Fair enough. I can't even imagine what it's like." She looked at the bedframe waiting to be assembled and the backpack still resting where Sara had left it. "I still have her parents' information. I can do some digging at work. See if anybody is looking for her. If she has any family out there. If you want?"

"If I want…" It seemed a strange way of phrasing it and my hesitation felt stranger still. Either way, it wasn't really my choice. "This was always meant to be temporary. If she has family that can look after her, that's for the best. In the meantime, she should have her own space." I pushed off of the couch. "Do you have enough time to help me get this stuff built?"

Kea stood with a stretch. "You know I love assembling things." We set to work, falling into a rhythm of bickering over the less than ideal directions, handing bolts and tools across the way while balancing pieces of wood, and occasionally swearing.

"You and Emily talking?" Kea asked during a lull while I tightened another bolt.

"We haven't sat down and had a real conversation yet. I know. I know. We need to. She deserves that. We were supposed to have dinner tonight, but I think the day caught up to Sara and she needs to rest. We will get it rescheduled soon, I promise."

Kea didn't question me, just gave me a nod

and a pat on the shoulder.

"The world is going to hell in a handbasket," I said, straightening from my task.

"Am I hearing what I think I'm hearing, Bennet Smith?"

I chuckled and shook my head. "No. No, I don't think so. Don't get your hopes up. I'm not going to be joining any revolutions. But keeping in touch with family and friends, I think I can do that."

She smiled. "It doesn't always have to be guns and a blaze of glory. Sometimes, you just need somebody to look after those caught in the crossfire. Somebody willing to take the initiative to build their community and better their world. A revolution still needs somebody to take care of those just trying to survive. On whatever scale. Small or large." She lifted one end of the twin mattress up and I grabbed the other, setting it on the frame.

A knock on the door drew both our eyes.

Rap kissed me when I answered. "You needed help with something?"

I stepped aside, letting her in, suddenly very aware of the difference between our two apartments. My rundown furnishings and cracked walls. I rubbed the back of my neck nervously. "Yeah, I'm moving the living room around a bit. Probably didn't need to rope you into all this, but…"

"I'm glad to help," she cut me off. "Hey, Kea."

"Hey, Rap. You missed all the fun carrying this stuff up." Kea stretched her back, surveying the collection of furniture waiting to be placed.

Rap laughed. "I can't say I'm upset I missed out on all the manual labor." She winked at Kea before turning to me. "Didn't realize you had a kid."

"I don't. It's temporary."

"A temporary kid?"

"No." I shook my head, feeling suddenly flustered as I ran my hand through my hair. Why had I invited Rap over for this? "She's just staying here a little while until I can figure something out for her."

"Wastes take me. Is this how awkward all of your dates are?" Kea laughed unhelpfully.

"No." I shot her a dirty look before turning to Rap. "It's just… Sara is like me."

"You told her?" Kea sounded impressed.

"Of course I told her." As if a second date was natural, 'Oh, by the way, I'm a walking corpse,' territory.

"She's a Second Life?" Rap's hand found mine.

I nodded, eyes drifting to the bed now built in the corner. "I want her to have her own space. I just don't have it in this apartment. I was kind of hoping the two of you might have some ideas. I got some furniture."

"And I carried it up the stairs." Kea elbowed me. "You are welcome, by the way."

"I have said thank you several times already." I rolled my eyes. "What do you two think? Because, at some point, I want to get my room back."

"You gave her your room? You are a sweetheart, Ben." Rap kissed my cheek.

"Well, her parents just got murdered. Letting her sleep on a bed felt like the least I could do."

"If you had done the least, you would have left her on that street to come back alone. You did plenty more than the minimum." Kea squeezed my shoulder.

"I wasn't alone when I came back. Good thing too." I rubbed my neck.

Kea's hand remained firm on my shoulder. "That's me, the master of perfect timing." She dropped her hand and went to the small dresser, adjusting its placement.

"You were there when he came back?" Rap asked, moving to help Kea. She looked between us before her eyes widened. "Oh, shit. Wait. I didn't put it together. You even told me the shades nabbed you. That was you? The Bluebelt Riots."

"That was me."

"People were rioting for a week after…"

I nodded slowly. "I was asleep for most of

that but Kea told me after the fact."

Kea was watching me, knowing how deep my guilt around the riots ran. "Those riots were the only reason I was able to get to Ben. All the shades got pulled away to deal with the active threat."

"Glad we could help, I supposed," Rap mumbled. How many people had been killed in those riots? I could have died a second time with nobody the wiser. I wouldn't have minded. All those people would still be alive.

"Whatever you are thinking, Ben, cut it out," Kea warned. "You didn't cause the riots. Your murder was an inciting event for a lot of people, sure, but if it hadn't been you, it would have been some other patsy."

"Thanks for that."

"You know what I mean."

"Of course I know what you mean, you insensitive ass." I shook my head. "Back to the task at hand. What do you two think?"

Rap and Kea shared a look before turning back to the living room, a wide enough room to allow for a little segregating.

"I think we can make something work," Rap said, her finger tapping thoughtfully against her chin.

"And I think you need to go pick up your temporary kid," Kea said, nodding toward the kitchen clock. "Rap and I will get this place ready for her."

***

Kea and Rap had done good work. Drapes and dividers gave the corner a feeling of privacy and the twinkle of fairy lights and decorations I hadn't been the one to purchase made the alcove a cozy escape. It wasn't perfect. It never would be in my dingy apartment, but from the way Sara's eyes shone and the smile that broke across her face, I knew perfection didn't matter.

Moments before, Sara had been drooling on my shoulder, but at the sight of the room, the girl perked right up.

"For me?" Sara whispered.

"I wanted you to have your own space. Kea and my friend, Rap, helped get it all set up for you." I smiled at Rap where she stood beside the stove. A pot sat at a low simmer with a stack of bowls waiting ready at her side. As if they hadn't already done enough, Rap had even taken the time to pull together a dinner that filled the apartment with the delicious tang of spices and vegetables.

Sara's eyes darted to Kea then to Rap, gratitude glistening there. Then she wrapped her arms around my waist and hugged tight. "Thank you." The height difference and my lack of experience with children in general made my return hug an awkward, tentative thing, but she didn't seem to notice or care. She held on for so long before darting to Kea and finally Rap to give them both hugs.

Rap couldn't stay much longer, but the sparkle in her eyes and the way she looked at Sara and me as she dished out curry brought a warmth to my chest that had me forgetting the constant ache in my bones. She gave Sara an affectionate hug on her way out the door before kissing me on the cheek and murmuring, "See you tomorrow."

15

With the first Tuesday date marked in the records of time as a success, I had earned my Thursday. Whatever it was that kept Rap coming back, I wasn't going to prod too deeply into it for fear of bursting the dreamscape bubble. We were so new and so fresh. My last relationship has been volatile from the start. Me never really good enough. Her never really all that interested. By the end we were more two people bound together by a mutual desire to keep our friends and loved ones from pitying us in a breakup. Turns out, everybody had been rooting for the split.

Things weren't like that with Rap. She didn't care I lived as barely more than a squatter in a crumbling home. She didn't care I didn't have aspirations for a corporate climb. She didn't care that I was content riding the bus to get around rather than investing in one of the resource guzzling cars that zipped through the city. It was easy enough to hire a driver if I needed to get where a bus wouldn't go, but really, where was I going?

For some reason I found it a relief when Rap

had welcomed Sara to join us at the movie that night. I would always take a date alone with Rap, and Kea would have gladly stepped in to keep Sara company, but I also didn't want the girl to feel like a burden to be shuffled along whenever she wasn't convenient for me. And there was something that brought a smile to my face at how easily Rap thought to include the girl. Even if Sara was only a temporary guest in my life.

By the time we had made it home, Sara had started drooping, her head lolling on my shoulder as I carried her on my back. As pleasant a night as it was bringing her with us to the film, it was nicer still knowing how heavily her recovery would pull her into sleep when Rap and I took to my bedroom.

Rap barely gave me time to close the door before she was on me. And I obliged her in every way until finally we lay still in rest.

The sounds of the city were a constant din. The occasional honk of a horn, the more frequent whine of a siren, a shout, or the rise of laugher filtering up from the streets below. I was so used to them that they were nothing but a white noise as Rap and I enjoyed the peace of the evening.

"Is what Kea said true? Do you feel guilty for the Bluebelt Riots?" With her ear resting on my chest, I worried about what she heard beating below. Some sort of arrhythmia?

Something not quite human? Something off? Or was I exactly the same now as I had been before dying?

I trailed my fingers up her spine, considering her question. She waited, patient as ever.

"She's right. It could have been anybody. A true member of the revolution or another innocent fool caught in the wrong place at the wrong time. But it was me. My death was the match that lit the brush fire of the revolution."

She pressed up on her elbow to look down at me. "Ben…"

"How many people died in Bluebelt? How many people were radicalized by my murder? How many took up guns? How many continue to die?"

"The city was a tinderbox waiting to ignite. There was only so much we could endure before we struck back."

I nodded. "But it was me and thanks to whatever strange wind blew in that day and brought me back, I have to live with that knowledge. That when the shades strung that rope around my neck and let me drop, people took to the streets and people died. My life wasn't worth that. I am not worth that."

She studied me for a long moment. "What about Sara? Would her life be worth it? Or her parents?" Her words were soft, her eyes beseeching. "The state would have continued spiriting us away, torturing us, killing us; and we would have continued to let them. At least now we are fighting back."

"Fighting back against an amorphous blob. What is the goal? Wipe out the top and more just like them step in. They tighten their grip. More die. Nothing changes."

"We don't let the top take the reins again."

I blew air out through my nose. My hand stilled on her hip. "From everything I have seen of this revolution, there is nobody set to take the lead. There is no direction except for destruction. Even if I agreed that wiping out the top was the solution, there is nobody set to fill the vacuum and I'm afraid of what chaos is going to rush in." I shook my head. "I don't know. I just want to be allowed to live my life. I want to be able to go outside and not have to worry about being dragged off to interrogation. I want to be able to take you out and not worry about some idiot getting trigger-happy."

"You shouldn't have to worry about those things. That's the point of all of this. You might have been the match, but Ben, Zenith needed a match. Can I bring you to a meeting? Let you see what is really happening?"

"That's not really my crowd, but..." The beseeching in her eyes was too much. "I'll think about it, alright?"

She nodded, laying her head back on my chest. "Do you work in the morning?"

My fingers resumed their gentle stroking of her spine. "I do." We had yet to wake up together. I would have to adjust my schedule soon if she kept agreeing to see me.

"I'll look after Sara in the morning and walk her to school."

"You really don't have to. I can leave something in the fridge, and Emily…"

Rap set her palm on my chest. "I want to, Ben. It will be nice. Now get some sleep."

16

I hadn't expected Kea to meet me at the end of my shift. I handed her a mocha, hung up my apron, and joined her at one of the small tables around the cafe. I no longer noticed the hiss of the steamer or the rattle of the coffee bean grinder while Kea's eyes continued to flick toward the noise makers each time they fired. The music playing overhead disguised some of the harsher notes and helped sink the surrounding conversations into the background.

Kea sipped at her mocha, watching me as I sank into the seat across from her.

"To what do I owe the honor?" I smirked at her attire. The pantsuit I so rarely got to see. The woman looked every bit the hard-hitting journalist I knew she was. Dressed to be taken seriously during her investigations. I noted Jackie taking note of Kea from behind the bar before returning my attention to my friend.

She fished a folded note out of her bag and set it on the table in front of me. "Didn't take too much to dig up some information on Sara."

I frowned at the scrap of paper.

"She has an aunt. Some cousins. They live in Zenith. Got her name and number for you."

I looked from the paper to Kea, still not touching the note. "Thanks for looking into it."

She sat back, nodding.

"Is she looking for Sara?"

"There's no missing person's report, if that's what you mean. That's not uncommon these days. Not many people file them when the shades are involved in the shootout. Too scared of being tied to the incident." She thrummed her fingers on the tabletop, eyeing the note. "Doesn't mean she isn't looking. Maybe she's handing out flyers or stopping by their house. I didn't hit the pavement on this one." She pushed the sheet toward me with one finger and I dutifully took it, folded it once more and slid it into my pocket.

"You working something good today?" I asked, changing the topic.

Kea smirked. "I am always working something good these days. A city this size and this volatile, it's hard not to be." With the note securely in my pocket, she had relaxed back into her charming self. Her eyes flicked to the counter and Jackie. Her eyebrow popped. "Your friend…?"

"You are exactly their type."

"Noted." She grabbed a napkin, clicked her pen, and scrawled something on it. I didn't need to look to know it was her number.

"Can't take you anywhere."

Jackie swooped in to clear Kea's cup, something we usually didn't do. Kea handed them the napkin note with a lopsided grin. The picture of swagger and confidence.

I just shook my head and waited for their silent exchange to end.

Jackie meandered away and Kea sat back in her chair, eyes following them as they went. "Any plans tonight?" She asked before slowly returning her attention to me.

"Finally getting that dinner with Emily."

She gave me a nod of approval. "Good man. She's going to need to vent, get some things off her chest. She's going to try not to, but you know Emily. She processes out loud. You ready for that?"

"As ready as I can be."

"Good." She clapped me on the shoulder. "I gotta run. I've got an interview in Midtown to get to. Tell me how things go with your sister." She stood, cast a look at Jackie, and left.

17

I was supposed to be focused on my sister, but the note sitting in my bedside table continued to drag on my mood. I should have been happy. I should have called Gloria right as I was leaving work. I should have been thinking about the return to a childless life. But instead I had shoved the note down deep in my pocket, tossed it carelessly into my bedside table, pushed it from my mind when I stood outside the school, and not even thought of bringing it up as we walked to Emily's house.

Emily stared at me over our salads. "Sara is fine. The boys will look after her." 'The boys' including Emily's full-grown husband, Derek.

"I know. I'm not worried."

"She's a good kid, you know that?"

"I do. Not that I had anything to do with that."

"Maybe not, but she has been opening up a lot recently. Settling in. That has a lot to do with you. She told me you built her a room."

"I wouldn't quite call it a room." I nudged a

tomato with my fork.

"A girl needs her space. It's a room. She loves it."

I nodded, a sigh escaping me.

"Alright, Ben. Spit it out. What is it? Something is bothering you, I can tell. There's no point in trying to hide it."

I knew there wasn't. I had learned in our youth that Emily could be a pest when she wanted to be. If she wanted information, she would get it from me eventually. Best to make it painless.

"Sara has an aunt in Zenith. Kea got me her contact information. I just can't seem to bring myself to text her. I can't hit the call button. Something is holding me back."

Emily frowned at me. "You care for Sara. That's what's holding you back. But she has family. Her family needs to know she is alive. Does Sara know?" There was a sudden heat coming from my sister, a pent up emotion begging for release.

I shook my head.

"Tell her. It is not your choice to keep anything from her. You owe her the truth. And you owe her family the opportunity to find her."

"I just... I don't..." I ran my hand through my hair. "It's not that I am trying to keep her from them. Trust me, Em. I'm not. I just... I don't know how much trust to give them... In certain areas…"

She caught my meaning, her flaring temper abating momentarily. "Nobody needs to know. You found her in Midtown. Her mother had shielded her body, right?" I nodded. "That's all her aunt needs to know. People don't trust the authorities these days. It makes sense you would have tried to handle the matter on your own. Her aunt doesn't need to know every detail. Just the ones that matter."

"Alright. Yeah. No, you are right. You are always right." I stuffed a forkful of greens into my mouth.

"Not always, but frequently." She watched me. I could see her restraint slipping, but her eyes darted around the restaurant and the other patrons. There was only so much that could be said in such a public place.

"I'm sorry," I said quietly between bites.

"You keep saying that, Ben, but I don't think you fully understand what we went through." Her lips pursed as the server cleared our salads and set down our entrees. Her eyes followed him as he retreated away. "It wasn't just the… the spectacle. It wasn't just watching it and knowing. It wasn't just the mourning that I was forced to do in silence. It's why it needed to be silent. Nobody could know there was a connection between me and that person on the television and what came after.

"I woke up in cold sweats, terrified *they*

would come knocking. Come asking questions. Tie you and me together and make my family suffer for the relation." She reeled herself in again, eyes once again scanning the restaurant to see if anybody was listening. "I still do sometimes."

I ran my fingers over my fork, lifting it to try to make this conversation look normal from the outside. The server asked how our first bites were and we both answered with an over done "Delicious," and our meals still untouched.

"Then to have Kea be the one to tell me… It hurt, Ben. And it's frustrating because I can't even be mad at you. I can't begin to imagine what you went through. I mean… I saw what they did to you. And then… I…" She swallowed. "I wanted to be there for you. But you didn't want me. And it hurt." She deflated back into her seat.

My fork lowered back to the table.

"It's only been the two of us for so long." She said in a near whisper. "Then you were gone. Gone like mom and dad." Her eyes raised to mine, her teeth worrying over her lip. "How long did it take us to even be told they were gone?"

"Too long." One day, they had left to spend some time alone together. Then they had just never come back. And there was Emily and I, wondering where they had gone and why they had left us. When the authorities had finally gotten around to informing us, the officer had done so with blasé airs and an assumption we already knew they had been killed in a hit and run.

18

Before my death, I hadn't been happy. During my death, I certainly hadn't been happy. After, it had only gotten worse. Now, the lightness I felt in my chest could almost be described as... joy? Maybe that was too strong a word for it. Connectedness? That seemed more fitting. I felt connected to the world in a way I never had before.

Nightmares still came. But now, instead of images of my body twisted and broken, my fears seemed to manifest in having my sister or her children disappear. Kea killed. Rap injured. But mainly, what made me wake up in a cold sweat was the thought of Sara being pulled away from me. Either the government's scientists getting their hands on her for research. Or some long-lost relative finding her.

When I managed to pull myself out of yet another nightmare, I found myself rolling to my side. I opened my bedside table and withdrew the scrap of paper that constantly haunted me. The name Gloria and a phone number. My fingers itched to shred the paper into unrecoverable flecks. But I knew it wasn't mine to shred. I needed to get ahead of this.

I stared at the paper until the sun came up, too restless with my decision and the rush of fear it brought with it. Standing, I padded out to the kitchen, trying to be quiet and let Sara sleep.

I set the scrap of paper on the table and turned to start on the eggs.

It wasn't long before Sara emerged from her curtained cove. She spared me her customary groggy glare as she woke up for the day before wandering into the bathroom.

I plated the eggs, setting the dish and a fork next to the note, and sat across from Sara's chair. She emerged from the bathroom looking refreshed with her freshly washed face, but still with a hint of sleep in her eyes.

She sat, grabbing her fork with a yawn that triggered a yawn of my own. It wasn't until the second forkful that her eyes found the note, reading the name scrawled there. Her brow furrowed and her fork slowly lowered from her mouth. Her eyes flicked to me nervously.

"I found your aunt's number. I—"

"You want me to go?" She asked in a panic.

"No. No. Sara, no. I haven't called her. I wanted to ask you first."

She swallowed, averting her eyes as if she could avoid the conversation by ignoring it.

"Gloria is your aunt, right?" No response.

"If you don't want to call her, we won't, but Sara…" I beseeched her to look at me. She didn't. "She's your aunt. Maybe she would like to know you are alive."

She was quiet for a long time before standing and retreating back behind her curtains. I didn't push her. When she didn't emerge in time for school, I sent Emily a text that she wouldn't be in that day. The administrators barely kept track of the children in attendance anymore. It would be too much work with how often parents were keeping their kids home to avoid getting caught in the middle of one of the ever-increasing conflicts between the revolution and the authorities.

19

Rap's hand was warm in mine as she led me down dark alleys and quiet streets.

"Where are we going?" I asked, a feeling of apprehension in my gut.

"I told you. To meet some of my friends." She cast that beautiful soothing smile back at me and I felt a pattering in my chest that was not at all calming. I couldn't shake the feeling she was up to something.

Over the weeks we had spent every moment of overlapping free time we could scratch out together, a feat with our opposing schedules. Things were going strong. It was only when she asked if I wanted to meet her friends that I grew nervous. I didn't know if it was the social anxiety knocking, or if it was because I knew how radicalized her friends were.

Strong as we seemed, I still worried it would be my misstep that would shatter us. So I had swallowed, nodded, and followed her down to the streets.

The bar she led us to was a rundown hole in the wall, but there was plenty of foot traffic streaming in and out. Rap's gaze flicked around the street, sending alarm bells ringing in my ears. But when she put her hand in mine and drew me into the bar behind her, I didn't resist.

She led me to a sprawling table in the back of the dimly lit room where punks in tattered black denim laughed. At first, it was easy going, introductions and handshakes. But a few beers in and the crew started heating up.

The rhetoric was all too much for me. The macho chest thumping and self-righteous proclamations. It wouldn't lead to anything good and I was sick of being pulled into less than ideal situations.

Under my drink, a grenade had been scratched into the wood of the table. Rap squeezed my hand excitedly under the table. "Ben, tell them what happened to you."

I moved to take my hand back from Rap but she held tight.

"I'm going to go," I said quietly instead.

She looked at me in confusion. "Why?"

I glanced at the door. I had pined after this woman and here I was messing it up. But this was quickly going beyond my comfort zone.

"I just don't know that this is my crowd. I'm going to go," I repeated with a touch more conviction.

She frown and released my hand. "I'm just going to say goodbye to everybody. Alright?"

I forced a smile and nodded. "I'll meet you outside."

Stuffing my hands into my pockets, I shuffled out of the excitable gathering and into the quiet streets. I knew that being out at night was a good way to get pulled in for questioning, but between the smoke and revolutionaries filling the house, I needed a little breather.

A few minutes later, Rap set a hand on my shoulder.

"You alright?"

I nodded. "Yeah. Yeah. Just. That was a lot."

"I thought you would appreciate it. After what was done to you."

I swallowed and started walking.

"It must get you fired up thinking about it," she said with all the vigor of her friends. She was fired up enough for the both of us. I said nothing. "We can affect change, you know? This is the time. Everything is so fucked right now."

"Rhapsody," I said, grabbing her hand and grounding her again. "This is a bad time and a bad place to talk about this."

"We should not have to live in fear like this," she said, but I could see her subdue a little under reality. "We should not be tortured and killed merely for stating our concerns."

"But we are," I said with a swallow and a glance around. "Please. Stop. I don't want trouble for us."

She took a deep breath, a small look of pity in her eyes that withered me to my core.

I pulled her to a stop and into the shadows. "Do you know what dying did for me, Rap? It didn't make me want to fight. It didn't make me want to be shown off to gangs of revolutionaries." She frowned. "It made me never want to die again. It made me never want my friends and loved ones to go through what I did."

She took my hands pleadingly. "The only way to change that is to take a stand. Now. Before things get out of hand."

"Even more out of hand, you mean? Shit hit the fan a while ago. The protesters turned to revolutionaries. The counter movement turned into radicalized extremists. The government cracked down to try to slow the spreading dissent. In response: more dissent, right? More crack downs. More killing in the streets on all sides. Things have already gone to shit. Every action is met by a more intense reaction.

"What your friends were talking about in there, that would only add to the body count. Maybe some would come back. Maybe. It's all luck of the draw, if you can call it that. But the ones who return could be on either side. The dead could be children." I covered my face with my hand and squeezed my eyes shut. "When did that stop mattering, Rap? When?"

"It still matters," she breathed.

I straightened, jabbing a self-righteous finger back the way we had come. Back toward the headstrong revolutionaries. "Not to them. To them, all is justified if the end state is their success. Their way. Their rules. How many people see it that way? How many Utopian dreams are out there that don't quite go hand in hand with each other? If we continue the killing, what will be left?"

She pursed her lips. "You think there's a peaceful solution to this? How many protests have you seen turn to bloodbaths? How many attempted overtures have led to imprisonment and torture? We have tried peace. Sometimes violence is the only way."

I shook my head. "Then it will just continue to escalate." I looked around again and I could tell she wasn't so far gone to not feel the rising threat in our locale. "Let's get somewhere safer for this conversation."

With a tight jaw, she nodded her agreement.

We were only a few streets over before she spoke quietly, a touch of shame in her voice. "I thought... I guess I thought you would appreciate meeting them all."

"I want to meet your friends. I want you to want to introduce me to them. I don't want to be held up as a once dead spectacle, or a rallying cry, or an example of everything that can possibly go wrong going wrong. You said that it does not matter that I died and returned. That it doesn't make me different. So let me not be different."

She swallowed. "I'm sorry. I didn't think of it like that. I didn't think." She looked at her hands. "I was just so angry. I was angry for you and I wanted to share my outrage. I see how that reduces you, though. I see how I was wrong." She raised her eyes to mine. "I am sorry."

"I know you are," I said, not entirely ready to forgive the affront.

***

I didn't turn Rap away at the door, but for the first time, I wasn't entirely certain I wanted her to stay the night.

Sara peeked out at us when we walked in. She wandered over to me timidly, while Rap wandered to the bathroom. Sara's fingers were knit together in a nervous twist.

"You okay, Sar? Did something happen?"

"No. Just... Can you call Aunt Gloria? I think I want to see her."

My mouth went dry. Why did the request feel like a punch to the gut? Still, I smiled, nodded, and gave her shoulder a light squeeze.

"I'll call her in the morning." The corner of her mouth quivered up with uncertainty, but she echoed my smile. "Now, get in bed, kiddo. It's late."

20

Sara was shy. So bleedingly shy. But with an optimism glinting in her eye that made me hope I had done the right thing. It had taken Sara weeks to finally feel ready to see her aunt. Another week still for her aunt to be ready to see her.

Sara grinned when a pair of boys bolted past her, shouting for her to come play, but when Gloria greeted her with excitement and smiles, Sara cringed and gave her only a half-hearted hug. Her eyes dropped to her shoes, and she shifted nervously from foot to foot.

Gloria was awkward in the face of the girl's uncertainty. Suddenly, the woman's surety wavered, and a nervous energy pinged between the two.

"Why don't you go play with your cousins while I talk to your aunt, Sara?" I offered.

The girl leaped on the offer and bolted for the playground.

"Sara?" The woman looked from the girl to me in confusion.

I shrugged. "It's what she's been going by at

school. She suffered a pretty big shock. Took her a few days to say more than a few words. Not using her real name seems to be a comfort for her." I rubbed the back of my neck, suddenly concerned that I should have pushed her to go by Reagan again. Maybe I was enabling her to bottle up her trauma or something. We never really had talked about what had happened to her. I thought I was giving her space, but maybe that had been a misstep.

Gloria shook her head. "We all thought she was with them at the farmer's market. It was something they did as a family."

I swallowed, trying to gauge this woman. Reading strangers would never be listed as one of my strengths. It was failing me now, but I decided to take a chance with a small truth. This woman was Sara's family. Open minded or not, sometimes blood was all that mattered.

"She was there. Her mother shielded her." My fingers tapped anxiously on my hip.

Gloria took in the new information, her throat bobbing and a fresh shine in her eyes as she watched Sara with her cousins. "Jules would have done anything for Rae." Her voice shook. "I can't even imagine what she's going through. I... I don't know if I'm equipped for this." Her arms crossed protectively over her chest. She looked at me. "Thank you for looking after her. How did you find her? Were you there? What happened?"

I bit my lip. "I was in the area. Heard the commotion. The gunshots. I guess I just reacted."

"That was very heroic of you."

"The fighting had already moved off before I got down to the street." I led us to a park bench and settled in, watching the kids play.

Sara and her cousins seemed to have settled into a how life must have been before. Gloria's smile was tinted with sadness. "We used to meet up with Jules and Reagan on the weekends. We always wanted our kids to be close. Maybe it was irresponsible to bring the boys today, but the moment they heard her name, it became impossible not to bring them. They are so good together, aren't they?" She swallowed down her grief. "Rae looks just like Jules did when she was that age." She looked down at her hands. "I can't believe she's gone." Her gaze drifted back to Sara. "I can't believe we didn't have Reagan at her funeral." She shook her head. "We were all wondering what happened to her."

"It took her a few days to say more than a few basic courtesies. It was only when I brought her to school that she opened up."

Gloria's lips pursed. "A trauma like that, I can't even imagine." She swallowed. "Of all the people who could have happened across her, I am glad it was somebody good."

I nodded absently, watching Sara play.

"You didn't tell me how you got my number."

"I have a friend who is good at running that sort of information down. She helped me."

Gloria nodded, biting her lip. "I'm sorry I laid into you when you called that first time. I thought you were some sort of creep."

"As would any reasonable person."

"We really thought that the state had just misidentified her. That, in a few months, we would hear back that she had been killed right there with her parents. We didn't..." She trailed off in a way that brought my eyes back to her. No wonder she hadn't been looking for Sara. She had assumed her dead.

Sara ran up to me, flinging her sweatshirt into my arms with a happy laugh before running back to her cousins.

I slung the sweatshirt over my shoulders and returned my attention to Gloria.

Something in her demeanor had shifted. The frown on her face was new and deep set with thought. Her throat bobbed and the warmth from just a moment earlier was gone, replaced with something else. Confusion. Fear.

"You said she wasn't hit. My sister protected her."

I nodded, but her unease had me rocking back. There was no retreat on the bench.

"Reagan had a scar on the back of her arm

from falling off her bike. Big. Unmistakable. Unmissable." She looked at me, eyes running up and down, calculations in her eyes. "Jules protected her…" Her eyes closed and she shook her head. I bit my lip. "It wasn't enough, was it?"

I didn't confirm what she already knew, just watched her nervously. There were enough cases of Second Lifes that it was well known that the magic that brought us back was thorough in its work. Even if our bones still ached underneath, the scars we had acquired in our first lives were wiped clean.

The bob in her throat drew my eye. "It's so good to see her doing so well." Her delivery was too flat, too forced. Maybe she heard it too because she tried to cover with a smile, but the corner of her mouth twitched. She had guessed what Sara was, and she was terrified of it.

"I was there when she came back. I didn't know about the scar."

"You weren't going to tell me?"

"Because it doesn't matter. She's alive. She's healthy." I nodded toward where the children darted around the playground. "She's happy. Your children are happy to see their cousin. Her being a Second Life doesn't change anything about her."

She bit her lip, her leg jiggling nervously under her. "You were there…" Her eyes widened and snapped back to me. I could swear she scooted a little further from me on the park bench. "Are you one too?"

"I died at a different time, but I am." I scrutinized her every move of discomfort and the fear manifesting in anxiously twisting fingers. "Does her being a Second Life change anything?"

She shot to her feet, shifting from foot to foot and rubbing her palms on her pants.

"I don't know how to take care of one of them... one of you..."

"She is no different than any other child."

"Her diet isn't... I don't know... restrictive some way?"

"Not that she's told me. She seems to like eggs. Or she tolerates them because it's all I know how to cook. But she's no more complicated than any other kid."

"What about aging? Is she still going to age? How does the magic work? I mean... Magic. I can't believe I'm even saying that." She was spiraling. Questions continued bubbling to the surface that increased my wariness of leaving Sara with this woman. She was looking for an out. Any out. Simply because Sara had died once. "I just. I don't think I can do it. I wouldn't be able to take care of... of... one of them." She stood. "You seem to be doing a good job of it already. She's comfortable with you. And well, you already know how... um... well, how it all works with the way that you both are." She was backing away, clutching at her purse, eyes scanning for an exit. "Boys."

I stood. "I understand if you need time with this information. But if you walk away from your sister's daughter without so much as saying goodbye to her right now, then lose my number. I won't give you a second chance to hurt her."

Sara was jogging our way. A smile creased her face. "Auntie Glo, will you come swing with me?"

Gloria swallowed, her eyes wild as she backed away from Sara's beckoning hands.

"She was terrified to see you again. Terrified and so excited. You were a part of her childhood. You are her family. She was worried you would be able to see she was a Second Life, but you never would have known if it hadn't been for the scar. If you hadn't asked and I hadn't told you the truth."

"Then you shouldn't have told me." She turned, not acknowledging the waiting girl. "Boys, time to head home. Yes. Right now."

Sara's grin had melted long before the woman's turn. Her face soured, and she looked suddenly so much older. She hurried to my side, and I wrapped an arm around her shoulders.

"I'll swing with you," I offered.

She shook her head into my side. "Let's go home."

I patted her shoulder once and turned us for home.

***

For days, I didn't know if I had made the wrong decision. My emotions swung between anger toward Gloria and remorse for Sara. With the intensity of my emotions, I couldn't imagine what Sara was feeling.

I questioned having reached out to Gloria. Maybe I shouldn't have told her about Sara's death. Maybe I should have blamed the absence of the scar on one of the wild magic breaches that seemed to be more and more frequent. Maybe I should have said it was the byproduct of one of the tools in the hospital. Maybe I had known the woman would react negatively. Maybe I had wanted her to keep Sara at my side. If she had realized later on, would she have cast Sara aside when she had nobody?

When a single knock prefaced the sound of a key in the door, I hoped that maybe Kea's upbeat attitude would help Sara reemerge from the shell she had closed around herself once again.

"What's up, kiddo?" Kea asked as she walked in.

"Hey, Kea," Sara drawled. She grabbed her books and retreated to my room. That she didn't opt for the false privacy of her curtains was telling.

"She okay?"

I shrugged. "Not really. We saw her aunt."

"I'm guessing that didn't go well."

I shook my head.

"You alright if I go sit with her?"

"If you think it will help."

She gave my shoulder a squeeze. Kea knew what it was like to be rejected by family. Maybe the shared experience would help. If nothing else, Kea's presence alone had always been a comfort for me. Maybe it would be the same for Sara.

21

In an unexpected turn of events, life was somehow good. The run in with Gloria passed like a blip. How quickly the girl got over her disappointment in her aunt had me nervous, but after a week of sulking and frequent visits from Kea, she seemed happy enough. Healthy or not, it seemed she had decided to move on.

Sara settled into the routine of going to school. I could tell she was frustrated by how much the day still exhausted her, but she craved the time with kids her age and the learning offered. I did my part to help her with homework where I could, but found myself with my phone in my hand all too often as I called up my sister or Kea for backup or advice. We fell into the weekly tradition of having dinner with Emily's family. It was becoming commonplace for me to be walking home from an evening at Emily's with Sara riding piggyback, her cheek plastered to my shoulder as she slept.

Surprisingly, even things with Rap were falling into place. When we met her friends, she kept it small and conversation steered clear of my death. I didn't ask about her family and the wealth she kept hidden, and she didn't bring up the fact I was dead. It was a perfect harmony that I am sure any therapist would have told us was unhealthy, but for the moment, it worked. I clung to anything that worked. I clung to the normalcy of it. There had never been anything special about me. There would never be anything special about me. Dying certainly hadn't changed that.

Sara made my apartment more and more her home, which I found I loved. The handful of nights that Rap slept over and Kea or Emily hadn't swept Sara away, I wandered out of my room in the morning to find Rap and Sara at the stove. Rap had made it her mission to ensure that Sara knew how to cook more than scrambled eggs.

I wasn't going to complain. Sara was proving a deft hand in the kitchen, and the smile I always found on her face when she cooked was infectious.

Even Kea stepped into the role of cool aunt as if she were born for it. Sara hung on her every word. Whenever Kea was around, I found the two sitting with their heads close, speaking quietly to one another as if they were the only two people on the planet.

The only thing that didn't quite fit was the occasional feeling of being watched. The paranoid certainty that the man in the park was staring at me or the woman at the coffee stand was lingering a little too long.

Had we been spotted that evening with Rap's friends? Had my name finally triggered the authorities to check into the man they thought they left hanging in a courtyard?

I was being paranoid. I was a nobody. They were strangers. It was all in my head.

22

Another Thursday with Rap sitting beside me at dinner. Even with Sara at Emily's, we had opted to stay in, my overcooked pasta between us. Rap, at least, was a good sport about my lackluster attempts at improving my cooking. My eyes went to the clock, knowing she had to leave soon.

"I've been meaning to tell you, Rap, I know these meetings are important to you. I didn't appreciate being blindsided that first time—"

She abandoned her fork to grab my hand. "I'm still sorry about that. It wasn't the intent. I just wanted you to meet my friends."

I gave her fingers a squeeze. "I know. I know. What I am saying is, I am willing to go with you. I'm willing to listen."

"Really?" Her eyes lit up.

I nodded.

"You're not just doing this to keep an eye on me?"

"I would be lying if I said I wasn't a little concerned when you go to these things. Not that having me with you is going to keep you any safer. But the rhetoric at these meetings…

It has the potential to turn…" I shook my head. "I just get nervous. But that's not why I'm willing to go."

She sighed. "If you are willing to come with me, I won't say no. I would rather have you with me, regardless of why. Just try not to pick any fights. Please."

"I'll do my best."

***

"You're that Second Life, right?"

Not even five minutes into another so-called 'community meeting' and we were off to the races. I had done my best to keep my head down and my mouth quiet during the last few, but that didn't keep Rap's ex from glowering at me each week.

"Ben." I offered my hand. It was almost a relief that he was finally confronting me.

Bekk grabbed it with a little too much emphasis, squeezing. "And you're dating Rap now?"

"I am." I squeezed back, not certain if Rap's ex was posturing or just inquiring. Maybe the too tight grip was just his norm. "Who told you I'm a Second Life?"

"We're a close-knit group here." He shrugged, his overgrown traps bulging in his tight black shirt. There had definitely been a flex in the movement, not that I could ever compete. "Everybody knows everybody's business."

"That's not business I told anybody except…" My eyes drifted to Rap.

Once again Bekk shrugged, but his eyes flicked to Rap for the briefest of moments before he remembered to release my hand. "Hey, Joey. Come meet this guy." He pulled his friend into a chest bumping hug before grabbing my shoulder and squeezing. "This is the guy the shades killed on national television. Bluebelt."

"Hey, man, let's not…" I said, eyes flicking around the room to see who had heard his booming voice. The answer was everybody.

"Nah, it's cool. No bigots here, man. We all got each other's backs." Bekk laid this assurance on me like it meant anything.

"What cell were you with?" Joey asked.

"Cell?"

"Of the resistance. Had to have been something big to have been given the royal treatment."

I shook my head slowly, edging out from under Bekk's hand. "I'm just a guy they scooped up off the street. Wrong place, wrong time."

"Not even a brother fighting for our future." Bekk shook his head, his face the picture of commiseration, but the mocking self-satisfied notes were unmistakable. "Just some dude.

You started this whole thing. You got people to pick up guns. You showed everybody the truth of how savage the shades have gotten. How much they want to silence us." His voice had risen again, bringing the room's attention back to him. "Your death was the trigger that mobilized the masses." His voice lowered back to be just between us. "And you are just some dude." He shook his head. "Nice that you got to come back, I guess. Not all martyrs do."

"Hardly a martyr."

"No. But you are a Second Life. Maybe you can't die. Maybe you can come back again." I didn't like the thoughtful little gleam in his eye.

"I hope not. I have already had the displeasure of dying once. What makes you think I would have any interest in trying it again?"

"You could be an invaluable tool of the revolution."

"No."

"But..."

"No." I repeated. "I don't like where this is going. So. No."

"You are being selfish."

"Have you ever died? Have you ever been killed? Gunned down and left in the mud to die. Only to find yourself in that same blood-filled mud, surrounded by corpses? Have you ever felt yourself be ripped open by bullets? Shot once, maybe? Extrapolate that out. I had six bullet holes in my body and a shattered pelvis when they finally hung me. Most people only have to die once. I wouldn't wish having to do it again on anyone."

"Maybe not everybody is as cowardly as you."

I shrugged. "Then ask them." I turned to walk away.

"I can't understand what she sees in you."

Same. But instead of admit it, without turning back to him, I said, "You can't understand why she sees it in me and not in you."

Rap followed me out, catching my arm and turning me when we were outside. "Ben?"

"Did you tell Bekk I'm a Second Life?"

"What? No." She rocked back on her heels.

"Then why does he know?"

"Your face got plastered across the nation. I'm sure Bekk didn't have to dig too far to figure out who you are." She had a point, and I instantly chastised myself for jumping on her.

I scrubbed a hand over my face. "Sorry."

She set her hand back on my arm, my attack already forgiven. "You okay?"

"If he thinks being tortured and killed is such an excellent tool for the revolution, then maybe he should try it. Who knows, maybe he will even come back a Second Life."

"You're being unkind."

I sucked in air and closed my eyes. "You're

right. It's just. It's my life. It's what happened to me and he is acting like he has some right to it. Like he owns it and can use it however he pleases. Like my death is just another bullet for his rifle. You know?"

Rap nodded solemnly. "Bekk can be kind of a dick. It's why we didn't work."

"He's not happy about that, is he?"

She shook her head. "I wouldn't say so. After he didn't say anything to us the last few meetings, I thought he was finally over it." She looked back toward the taproom. "He's made himself rather central in this group. If you want to go, we will go."

I hung my head, running my fingers through my hair and looking back toward the meeting. With beers in hand, people were starting to take their seats. "Like I said, I know these meets are important to you."

"It's not just for me."

"No. I know that. It's something bigger. I get that. I want to want to be here for you. I can't do it if my death is being held up like some... symbol or something. I'm nobody. I have always been nobody. I don't have any aspirations to be..." I waved my hand noncommittally. "Whatever it is they seem to want me to be. I certainly don't want to be some prop in Bekk's war campaign." I met her eye. "I don't know that violence is the answer here, and I'm worried that he is driving all other options out the door."

Rap took my hand, eyes beseeching me to see the truth. "Negotiations don't do anything. Not with the government. They are just a means for the shades to get more of our faces in their books for rounding up later."

"I know the negotiations are failing. That's not what I mean, though. We can strengthen our communities and make our lives better. Make the lives of those around us better, with or without the support of the government. We don't need negotiations. What we need are fewer bullets tearing through parks and playgrounds." I closed my eyes and squeezed her hand.

"The meetings are meant to discuss all options. You improved your building. Tell them about it. Let more of that spread. These are community meetings. Open forums and discussions. Bekk does not rule all in them."

My smile even felt pitying to me and I quickly tried to wipe the expression away before Rap took insult. "He has a terrible amount of sway. There's a lot of people in there flocking to bend to sentiment like his. Anybody who speaks up will just be talked over. We have both seen it. You've noticed, right, Rap? The way these talks always turn to violence. Fewer and fewer moderate minded folks have been showing up. The group is becoming radicalized and with Bekk driving them, they are becoming more aggressive and willing to take risks. Even discussing violence in an open forum. These meeting are not about community anymore."

She frowned.

"I'll go back in with you. Just don't call attention to me, please."

"I won't, Ben, I promise, but I can't promise anything about Bekk."

"I'm not asking you to."

She kissed my cheek, squeezing my hand. "It means a lot that you came."

23

I hadn't thought anything of it when my hair had grayed at the edges, nor the slow creep that overtook my whole scalp over the course of months. I was of an age where that was normal enough. When the first streaks of gray touched Sara's hair, though, that made me frown. She seemed young for it. But I wasn't an expert on kids. Maybe it was just how it went for some of them. Then I started noticing the pattern. And if I noticed the pattern, so did others.

It wasn't just us, it was all Second Lifes. We were fast to gray. Faster than the average person. The color leeching away from our hair was a swift transition to stark white. The moment I realized the hair was a side effect of death, I hurried to the store for a box of dye to add color back to Sara's locks. We were tolerated for the most part, but it was the curious scientists who spent their lives harnessing magic and the trigger-happy vocal minority I feared. Better to hide the obvious signs of our difference than to let something as simply fixed as our hair color give us away.

I wore my cap tight over my head as I ventured out, leaving Sara in the safety of our unit with her homework. If she needed anything while I was out, Farah was more than happy to have her visit. When had our building become such a community?

An older woman eyed me as I surveyed the boxes of hair dye. I was too suspicious. I needed to be decisive. I needed to move. With the number of bodies in the streets, there were too many people coming back from the dead these days to go unnoticed and the masses were starting to get uneasy at the frequency of wild magics within the city bounds. Everybody was getting twitchy. The stark lights beating down on us in the sterile white aisle brought beads of sweat to my brow.

I reached for a box at random, landing on some red tinted variation on brown, and turned to hurry away. A gentle hand set on my shoulder before I made it very far. I turned slowly, my throat bobbing with a nervous swallow. Had I been made?

The woman took the box from me with a shake of her head, setting it back on the shelf before replacing it with a soft brown. "Go with something lighter. Transition slow, but it's easier to hide the gray in blonde. The roots are less noticeable. It's your beard that will give you away if you let it grow out." Her voice was a quiet secret between the two of us. She gave me a knowing look. "Go to a few shops around town and get a stock going."

She turned to go, but stopped. With a glance around, she dug in her purse, pulling out a small notebook and a pen. She scratched out a note, then tore out the page and handed it to me. "Days are getting dangerous. It's time for us to pull together." She nodded to herself and ducked away.

My eyes followed her before looking at the note. *Call me.* Innocuous enough if it was found on me.

I took the woman's advice, picturing Sara's amber brown hair and picking one a few shades lighter still. I circled the store until I was sure the woman was long gone, snagging a few snacks for Sara and I before heading to check out.

***

Rap stopped by to help with Sara's hair. While the dye set, Sara plopped onto the couch to watch trash TV while Rap and I retreated to the kitchen. Rap's prowess in the kitchen was rubbing off on me, and I had started trying my hand at making more than eggs and unevenly cooked pasta for dinner.

Rap's arms wrapped around my waist, her chin popping up onto my shoulder. "Call me?

Oo-la-la." She joked, spotting the note sitting to the right of the stove. "Run into somebody cute at the pharmacy?" She pinched my butt and nipped my neck.

"If you are into older ladies." I turned off the stove and turned to face Rap, my own arms joining hers in our embrace. "Pretty sure she's a Second Life. Said we should pull together."

"Probably a good idea for you all to have more of a network." That she said it quiet enough to keep Sara from hearing had me narrowing my eyes at her.

"What have you heard?"

"Nothing really. Just some rumblings among the patrons at work."

"Like?"

"It is stupid stuff, Ben. Like, with people not dying 'like they ought to be, there's no jobs for the living.' Very illogical garbage. But angry people are willing to believe illogical garbage." The timer for Sara's dye sounded, ending our conversation for the moment. "You should call that woman."

24

The woman's name was Claire. I questioned the wisdom of meeting the woman at her house, but I had to hope that if push came to shove, I could handle myself, spry as she had looked at the store.

The house was an old multilevel built long before the sprawl of the city had dominated the surrounding area. Somehow she had managed to retain a lot of land large enough to accommodate row after row of garden boxes.

The house was alive when I arrived. People coming and going. People sitting on the front porch chatting. People kneeling beside the garden beds quietly weeding.

Claire sat on the porch, sipping on a lemonade with a book resting open on her thigh and her free hand resting in the loose grip of the woman reading beside her.

I opened the chain-link gate, which emitted a small screech as it swung, drawing a few curious glances and smiles from the gardeners, and stepped into the bustle. Claire waved for me to join her, indicating the open chair beside her.

"There's a lot of people here," I commented as I took a seat, looking over the activity in the gardens.

"We've got a lot of roommates. And some of the local kids like the gardens." She angled to face me without dropping her partner's hand. "How long ago did you die?"

I swallowed, eyes darting around, uneasy with the open discussion.

She popped a half mouth grin. "Look around you."

I did as I was told.

"You start being able to feel it more the longer it's been, but I suspect you can discern the pull."

Not all the people coming and going were Second Lifes, but as I studied them, I came to realize that many were. Her hand slipped from her partner's as she followed my gaze with a nod.

"A lot of them are off the books these days. They were reported dead. Lost their ability to get housing without outing themselves, so we took them in." Claire turned toward me fully, eyes scrutinizing. "You're not alone, are you? You have somebody you're looking after. Strange thing, isn't it? Random as the wild magic seems, it doesn't tend to bring us back without a little help. I can already see you thinking about the moment. You were there when another Second Life was brought back."

There was no point denying it, so I nodded. "A little girl. Goes by Sara. Her parents were killed."

Claire nodded as if that all made sense. "Damnedest thing. I can't figure it out. If the rebirth magic is so wild, why does it seem to call out for help?"

"You don't think it's random?"

"Oh no. I do. I don't think there is any reason behind who and when and why. But I do think that we don't understand magic as well as we seem to think we do. I think we have grown a little too reliant on something we don't know a lick about and too confident in our abilities to harness it to power every aspect of our lives. There's no harmony in what we are doing anymore." Her eyes took in the city that rose all around her slice of sanctuary. "There is only domination." She shook her head.

I surveyed the rise of concrete and neon around us. It wasn't natural, but it was home. I'd never questioned any of it before. The way the scientists harnessed and tamed magic. The way the developers built and paved over every inch of the natural world they could, leaving only small wisps of close cropped green in the parks. The way everybody flocked to those green spaces to touch an approximation of the natural world.

"I'd like to meet her sometime, if you are

comfortable with that. It's got to help, having a few people who know what it's like." She looked back toward her partner who had set down her book. "I'm being rude. This is my wife, Isabella. Ben. Met him at the pharmacy the other day." We exchanged friendly smiles and nods. Another Second Life. "We came back together. Never met before that day, but we came back together. Found each other before the baggers came round. Both of us were in rough shape, as you may imagine. Had to lean on each other to get off the streets. Been together ever since." She grinned, her love for the woman painted plain in her eyes. "I guess that's not the most romantic of love stories."

"There's a beauty to it," I said quietly, eyes roving the commune. "I think Sara would like to meet you all."

25

After months of attending meetings with Rap, it was clear that the violence was only going to increase. That, for some members of the group, collateral damage was the cost of revolution. Earlier meetings had felt more like an airing of grievances, a safe space to complain with little actual action spilling out of it. Now, I hated to admit, but Bekk was fully at the helm and he was steering the ship away from venting and small actions.

As always, Bekk was at the front, speaking. Ranting was more like it. His fist slamming into his open palm to emphasize his displeasure. There was something so contrived about the way he sat, lounging on his stool at the head of the space to bring himself more level with the rest of the attendees. He didn't fully sit, though, allowing his natural height to elevate him ever so slightly above the others.

"We were out on the streets, recruiting and speaking truth to word, and some little shit had the audacity to tell us to get a job. It's like nobody cares anymore."

"I think we have a few more important things to think about than your ego," I grumbled. When I realized all eyes had turned to me, I shrunk momentarily under their scrutiny. Rap nudged my knees lightly under the table, a silent prompt. "We have entire colonies of people who got forced from their homes and shoved out to die in the wastes. Children getting gunned down beside their parents at dog parks and farmers' markets."

"Jackasses who think they are heroes just because they got misidentified as a rebel and tortured to death for a cause they don't believe in," Bekk sneered.

"Yeah, those too," I said, owning my pointless death. "And jackasses who think the rallying cry of a movement meant to change this world should be their own whining over being insulted in the street by some kid. Not everybody is going to get behind you. Not everybody is going to think the sun shines out your ass. People believe the shades are doing the right thing. That their rule of force is necessary to keep the crazies in line and the world from collapsing. To them, those crazies who threaten their lives are us. You can't win this by crying in the corner that not everybody likes you and lashing out against innocent bystanders to prove some sort of point. You don't save the environment by burning down the forest.

"So yeah, I got killed in the crossfire of a fight I had no place in. Yeah, I lived my life not getting involved in the cause. Not because I don't believe we need change, but because the cause you all chant about, all it's done is get people killed and tighten the stranglehold. Not all of us killed get the chance to stand back up again." I said grimly, standing as I spoke. I left the room with Bekk fuming at my back and a trail of eyes following me. For a second I wasn't certain if Rap would follow me, but a moment later she scrambled up behind me.

She shoved her hands into her jacket pockets and swore. "You are not wrong about his ego. But you are not right either."

I shook my head, not in the mood for whatever this fight was going to be. I had made a mistake in coming.

"I don't understand why you don't care," she said.

"It is not that I don't care. It is that I don't think the way you are all going about this is right." I bit my lip. "How many innocent people is Bekk willing to sacrifice? Is he even trying to mitigate the damage he does anymore?" I met her eye. "Maybe the more important question to ask is: What is your line? How many are you willing to sacrifice? Not all of us come back." I swallowed and looked back toward the restless crowd. "These discussions are taking a sinister turn. I don't like it. And now Kea is disappearing at night."

"The shades have made it clear that there cannot be progress without a strong arm."

"I don't want you or Kea to be that strong arm."

"Somebody has to be."

"What if you get yourself killed?"

"What if I do, Ben?" Her frustration came out barking and she sliced her hand through the air between us before her expression turned beseeching. "You should care more than the rest of us! You should be the most willing to fight!"

"I already died once. What else do you want from me?" I demanded. "I got a second chance. I took a breath I never thought I would. Now you think that just because I went down in a hail of gunfire that I am raring to go charging headlong into another wall of bullets. Not at all. Not in the slightest. If you really think that is the type of person I am, you mis-assessed."

"Yeah. I did." She turned on her heels and walked away.

I didn't go after her. She would get herself killed and me along with her. There was no future there. There was nothing there but death. I hadn't been the radical revolutionary before and I certainly wasn't one now.

For the first time, I had somebody counting

on me, and it wasn't Bekk and his revolution. I needed to get home to Sara. I needed to get home to my daughter.

26

I yawned, sprawled out on the couch in a way I no longer had the opportunity for with Sara around. Claire had the kid out working on knot tying or gardening basics or some such. The girl had taken to the older woman and her cohort of Second Lifes. She had gone so far as to start calling them the Aunties. An endearment Claire and Isabella seemed to welcome. The Aunties seemed good enough people, aside from their survivalist tendencies. Without Rap around, and Kea out more and more often, I was just glad that Sara had found more people to trust.

Rather than some trash game show, I had opted for the news. Honestly, it was about the same amount of entertainment, but with twice the terror at the knowledge that what the newscasters reported was true, at least in part. Another protest. Another riot. Another instance of the vocal few creating chaos for the masses. At least that's what they said.

I didn't bother listening if it was Zenith or

some other city. They were all starting to look the same.

I had been to enough of the meetings to know that the vocal few didn't care how many of the peaceful protesters they pulled into their line of fire. They saw opportunity in the shades taking innocent bystanders in to be tortured. They used it as righteous fuel.

I had seen enough trigger-happy kids on the street and I had seen how much blood they could get flowing in only a matter of moments. I had seen how quickly terrified kids in uniforms could bring their weapons to bear. I had seen how ruthlessly the shades put down injured survivors caught in the crossfire. Easier to have them dead and silent.

I let my eyes close, still waiting for the knock that would signal Claire and Sara's arrival, absently listening to more of the drama unfold on the newscast.

"Authorities are looking into the rampant spread of rebirth wild magic that is sweeping through the city." My eyes snapped open. "An increase in Second Lifes has been noted in recent years. The authorities believe the rise in power fluctuations and failures of small magics around the city is tied to the increase. They also suspect that several of the body thefts that have occurred of executed rebels have actually been instances of Second Life rebirths. Most instances of rebirth have been noted amid rebel populations. Authorities have released photos of all rebels whose bodies have been stolen following execution. These individuals are considered highly dangerous and should be reported immediately."

I was sitting, eyes glued to the television as a series of seven photos blinked by in slow procession. Mine was some terrible photo captured years before. I remembered when it had been taken. I'd been half dead, dragged in and propped up. I hoped that the color drained from my face, my shaggy hair, and bruised cheek were disguise enough. I hoped nobody watched the news. I hoped nobody cared.

I remembered the watchers.

"Authorities believe that the recent surge in Second Life rebirths may be at fault for the wild magic disruptions breaching the outer city from the wastes and urge extreme caution when interacting with suspected Second Lifes until we have a greater understanding of the situation."

My phone buzzed. I let it ring through. It buzzed again. I numbly brought it to my ear.

"I think the authorities just called open season on Second Lifes," Kea said in a hollow voice. "Please tell me you are somewhere safe."

"Home. Sara… Sara is on her way with Claire."

"Nobody knows about her. There's no reason to suspect it from looking at her." Still, I didn't miss the note of panic. "She's going to be fine."

"Gloria…" I said in a thin whisper.

27

I reduced my hours, adjusting my shifts to be with Sara anytime she wasn't at school. Her routine no longer included playdates, not that many parents were taking the risk these days. She went to school. I walked her home. She stayed in while I ran errands. It wasn't a life, but the risks weren't worth it.

I tried to look casual and unconcerned by the men drinking beers in front of a rundown apartment building. I hoped I would pass unnoticed while they joked. There was a risk in avoiding the busy streets these days, but also a risk in walking them.

"You look like a Second Life." The growl in the words told me it was a threat as the man approached. He smacked his buddy's shoulder, bringing his whole small pack into the conversation. "What do you think? Is he one of them?"

"I don't know. He's gray like one."

"Man, I'm coming up on forty. Give me a break." I said, trying for casual as I took a step to the side to maintain space between us. I had become good at streaking color through my hair to make the gray look more natural, but I was quickly coming to realize assholes would jump on anything. My hand tightened on my grocery bag as if it would prove much of a defense.

The men straightened off of the car they lounged on and started walking over. They had decided long before that their day would contain violence. I just happened to be the easy target that walked by. I tried not to panic, keeping space between me and them as they stalked after me in pursuit. Maybe if I could make it somewhere a little better lit, a little better trafficked, I could escape, or maybe the opposite. Maybe they would be able to convince a mob to join in.

I stood my ground, but couldn't keep my feet for long.

I tucked my arms around my head and neck in meager protection and curled into a ball. Their kicks and stomps brought crushing pain to the surface, but worse were the memories. The torture. The broken bones and flayed skin. This beating was nothing compared to that. As long as they stopped.

When I didn't fight back, I think it took the excitement out of the abuse for the gang. Steadily the kicks stopped, petering out to insults and laughter, before the men upended one of their beers over me and the pack returned the way they had come for more drinks.

I lay in a bloody heap tucked in against the wall and the street and waited for who knows how long before I managed to unfurl my limbs. Using the wall for support, I got to my feet, pulled my hood over my head and hobbled toward home.

My fingers were shaky and fumbling, but managed to draw my phone out of my pocket. My first instinct was to call Kea, but I knew she was on a date and I would hate to be the one to disturb her. Instead I called Rap. I hardly wanted her to see me like this, but I knew I needed help.

"Ben?"

I forced what strength I had into my voice, trying to ignore the pain that shot through my ribs when I did so. "Hey, Rap. Sorry to bother you. I… I might need a little help at home if you are free tonight."

"I have a shift, but I can come by after?" She sounded uncertain, clearly having picked up on something in my voice. Maybe the waver or rising winces of pain with each step.

"After is fine," I said, hoping a shorter sentence would draw less attention.

"I'll get Tanner to cover for me. He wants the hours anyway."

"No. No. After is fine, Rap."

"I'm coming over." That was that.

I had called for help. Why was I being so

difficult in receiving it?

The building was quiet enough when I walked in. I was almost to my door when Farah popped into the hall with her youngest. The woman's eyes widened when she saw the blood on my face and the way I clutched at my ribs. She rushed back into her unit, the door closing behind her with a heavy thwack.

My dexterity failed me as my shaking hands failed to sink my key into my door's lock. I tried again only to be rewarded with my keys slipping from my fingers.

Before I could stoop to pick them up, another hand drew them up. Rap must have left as soon as I had called to be here so soon. She took one look at me before jingling the keys in the lock. Her arm wrapped gingerly around me and she helped me into my unit. Before the door could close, Farah stepped across the threshold with a cobbled together medical kit.

"I just live down the hall," Farah said by way of greeting to Rap before hurrying to help me down onto the couch.

Sara sat wide eyed at the table, her homework spread out in front of her all but forgotten. Farah took one look at the girl and beckoned her over.

She bent to meet Sara's eye. "I'll get your dad cleaned up and we will get him taken care of. I need you to look after Fausti and Jidi. Can you do that?"

Sara's eyes were glued to me while Rap helped me to sit.

Farah drew Sara's attention back. "While I take care of him, I need you to watch my boys. Can you do that?" She repeated, her voice firm.

Sara gave a rapid nod; her eyes crinkled with a mix of fear and concern before she darted off.

"Maybe I should bring him to the hospital," Rap said when Sara was away.

"You cannot bring him to the hospital." Farah said with such suddenness that both me and Rap stared at her. She set her medical kit on the table beside me while Rap dabbed at my wounds.

"What do you mean, I can't bring him?" Rap asked, incredulous.

"She's right," I said slowly, casting Farah a sidelong look. "I can't go to the hospital." I was wary, but something in Farah's eyes told me she knew what I was. "I don't know what their instruments will see when they look at me."

Rap shook her head in confusion, looking between Farah and me. "You have a pulse and vitals. I can't imagine it's any different for you than others."

"I would have thought the same until I realized sniffers can't see us. Something to do with the small magics that went into their creation, maybe."

"Wait. Sniffers can't see Second Lifes?"

Rap's eyes widened with an excitement that set me on edge. "Do you know what that could mean?"

"Right now, I don't really care what it could mean for the revolution."

"Right. I'm sorry. I just…" She caught herself and returned to bandaging the open gashes and cuts.

Farah eyed the woman with a sudden unease before her attention returned to me.

***

Rap stayed after Farah left. I heard her talking with Sara, issuing her assurances about my health, and telling her she would stay the night just in case. Sara peeked in on me in my room to confirm Rap's words. She favored me with a wavering smile before ducking away just as quickly.

Rap sat with her a little longer before coming in to sit beside me on the bed. Her fingers curled lightly around mine. "I miss you, Ben."

"I miss you, Rap."

She swallowed. "I've been wanting to apologize. That night, I was heated from the meeting."

"I think we both were." I groaned as I shifted, my ribs protesting. "We have different goals."

"Do we really though? Do we have to? Not everybody needs the blazing glory of guns and a street fight, but look at your building. Look what you changed in this space. Look at the community you helped shape. With a small act. Multiply it. And keep multiplying it. Each of us has a place in this. We need the peaceful progress to shape the community just as much as we need the violence to route the oppressors."

I smiled sadly, settling into my pillow and studying Rap. "And there it is again."

"What?"

"You don't want to help me build a community. You want to take down the state. We are on two very different sides of this."

"And we need both sides. That's what I'm saying."

"So, what? You want me to build a community? Pull people together peacefully, but always with the fear that they will get caught in the crossfire of this revolution?"

"There won't be crossfire forever. Once the state has been brought to heel, we can fall back into our communities. It is a necessary evil for the time being. War always is."

I sighed. "Did you hear yourself say that just now? Like it or not, you're following Bekk, and Bekk doesn't want people to pull together. He wants them scared because only when they are scared are you able to recruit more trigger pullers for this war. Only when they are scared is he able to justify this violent opposition. Bekk's bombs are hitting military targets, yeah, but there's a strategy there. Maybe you don't see it. But there is. Bekk doesn't give a shit about the civilian populace. He doesn't care about the communities."

"What are you talking about?"

"Look at what happens after every bomb. The shades take to the streets. They aren't killing revolutionaries, are they? Just open your eyes and look at what follows. Guns, more killing, harder crackdowns; but the revolutionaries have already cleared the scene. Sure, there's enough to kick up some dirt and cause a ruckus. Enough to get those officers pulling triggers. Enough to record the fallout."

"You think that Bekk is intentionally catching civilians in the crossfire?" She said in disbelief, her hand snapping back from mine. "I know you hate him. He was never the best boyfriend, but he's not a complete asshole."

"I am just saying, look at what is happening. Maybe he is not. Maybe it is not intentional. I can't say. But what I do know is that the first explosion was a car bomb outside a government center on a Saturday. Why a Saturday? To limit casualties? Maybe. Or maybe it was something else." The memory of the crushed flowers under Sara's father's body was stark in my mind. "Either way, I don't think we are on the same path. I don't think we ever will be. And if you tell Bekk that sniffers can't detect Second Lifes, then I would never be allowed to just build community. For me to do the right thing, the right thing for Sara, would be for me to leave."

"You would just run away?"

"For Sara, I will do anything that keeps her safe. Being here. Letting people plot and scheme about how to use Second Lifes to further their cause when we are already being murdered in the streets is not a way to keep her safe."

"If we never take action, it will never get better. Tomorrow will never be better."

"I know. And I get it. But I'm not the man for it. That's not me, Rap. It is never going to be me. I don't want it to be."

"You are scared. I get it. But you were brought back for a reason."

"That's just it. There was no reason behind it. It was a random occurrence. That's what wild magic is, a series of random occurrence. It doesn't mean anything. It doesn't make me special."

"That's because you refuse to try. You refuse to be special." There was a note of pleading in her voice.

I shook my head. "It's not that I refuse to be. It's that I don't want to be. I want to forget that any of *that* ever happened to me. I want to move on with my life, shitty and menial as you think it is. I want to be around to take care of Sara. I don't want a target on her back. And if there is one on mine, there is one on hers. Can you understand that, Rap? I'm content with my small, pointless life, if it means I can give anything at all to Sara."

"Then give her freedom."

I closed my eyes and shook my head. I blew a long stream of air out between my lips before opening my eyes once again. "I hope one day we have that. I hope there is a day where we don't have to worry about a gunfight breaking out on the street. I am hopeful, Rap. But I am not going to be the one who brings that change. And frankly, I know that this is all going to get a lot worse before it get's better. I can't be a part of that."

"Then you will be complacent in it."

I shrugged. "I have my priorities, and getting strung up on national television for a second time isn't one of them. Getting lined up in front of a firing squad isn't one of them. That's where this road you want me to be on leads."

Her disappointment burned into me.

"Thank you for coming when I needed help."

"Of course, Ben. Anytime. But don't make getting your ass kicked a habit, please. I'll get you some water and some painkillers. Get some rest. I'll just be in the living room." She kissed my cheek and stood. At the door, she stopped. "I trust that whatever you do, you will keep her safe."

28

Claire didn't look the least bit surprised when I showed up at her door, nor at the state of my bruised and battered body when I did. She ushered me into her house with a quick scan behind me.

"You look like you've got something big to share."

"We are leaving, Sara and I."

She nodded. "Good. Because so are we. I have gear enough for us to get established out there."

"You're planning on running to the wastes?"

"It's the safest place for us now. You and the girl are welcome to join us. I was hoping you would, actually."

"The wastes are dangerous."

"Who told you the wastes are dangerous?" She asked with a smirk. "The newscasters who give their voices for the authorities? Think about it. It's all propaganda. It keeps the population centralized. It keeps the unknown magics alien and at bay. We tend to forget that people used to live out there happy as could be."

"People who had the skills for it."

"We've got them. We learned them. We've been teaching Sara, and we can teach you." She seemed so confident it was hard not to trust her words. Maybe it was possible. She covered my hand with hers, catching my gaze and holding it. "I saw them burn a woman today. They thought she was one of us. I couldn't even tell you if she was. I didn't feel that pull, though. They tied her up and burned her alive on a suspicion. Burned her so she couldn't come back."

"The shades did that?"

She shook her head. "Just people, hon. People." She swallowed, eyes growing distant with the memory. She sharpened once again. "We are getting out before this gets worse. You should come. If not you, send Sara. She's young, quick, and malleable. She'll do well out there. She'll have us to look out for her."

***

Kea kicked her feet up when she stopped by. She looked ready to settle in for a nap on the lounger while I finished prepping dinner, but then she frowned, sitting up straight and alert. She scanned the room, taking in the stuffed framed backpacks by the door. "Going somewhere?"

"The Aunties are thinking of getting out of town."

"And you are thinking of going with them."

"It's not safe in Zenith. It hasn't been for a while. But…"

She nodded, understanding. "The government is blaming Second Lifes for the wild breaches, the bombs, the revolution, everything that makes life dangerous, or even vaguely uncomfortable. Worse, they are supporting it when Second Lifes are subjected to a mob. The city is not safe for you," she agreed.

"It's not safe for anybody. If your hair grays too early. If you walk a little funny. If you look at somebody the wrong way."

Her lips pursed, and she set her hand on mine. "You're my brother, Ben."

I didn't like her tone, the softness in it.

"That's why I'm asking you to come with us. If we go… When we go. Come with us. Please, Kea. Sara loves you. I love you. We both need you."

She squeezed my hand, and we both held tight to each other. "Things are heating up, Ben. We are at a breaking point and I need to be here for it. Somebody needs to tell the story. Somebody needs to be in the streets fighting. That's the only way we can be certain this breaking point is a turning point."

I swallowed, fear coursing through me for my best friend. "You live like you don't have to be afraid of dying. Well, dying fucking sucks. I don't want you to experience it until you are good and old and it's your time to go. I want you to come with us."

"Look. I want that, but if I don't fight, then nobody gets to have that future. Nobody gets to die peaceful and happy except the ruling elite. We will keep getting gunned down in the streets. Kids will keep getting murdered and being labeled terrorists. The propaganda machine will keep churning out directives to eliminate anybody they don't like. If I don't fight, then who does? And why should they have to put their life on the line if I am not willing to? This is what I keep trying to tell you, Ben. I respect that you want to be separated from it all to protect Sara, but you aren't really separate. Nobody is." Kea set her hands on my shoulders, looking me square in the eyes as she willed me to agree with her. "I don't want you to fight, Ben. I want you to take Sara and keep her safe, because I want her safe. I want her to have the future that was so nearly stolen from her. But the only way I can give that to her is to stay and fight."

I fell back into my chair, deflated. She rose, setting her hand lightly on my cheeks as she bent to kiss my forehead. She continued to hold my face as she straightened. "I want you to take her and go. Get out of this city. Circle up with the other Second Lifes and take your chances in the wastes."

29

Kea had left for the evening to do who knew what anymore. Nothing good, I suspected. When she had said her farewells to Sara, holding the girl so tight, it had felt final. Sara was young, but she wasn't stupid. She clung just as tightly.

I knocked on Farah's door. The rustling I heard moments before went silent. The quiet approach of feet on the creaking wood floor reached me through the door before it cracked ever so slightly.

The woman standing inside looked terrified, eyes wide and wild. Her throat bobbing as she surveyed the hall with fresh anxiety. She gestured for her kids to duck around the corner before pulling me in and bolting the door behind me.

"Are you alright?" I asked.

"No. No. I am not. And you are not either." She paced anxiously. "I'm getting my children out of this city, and you should, too. What they did to you on the street was just the start." Her voice was an anxious whisper. With a glance behind her to make sure her kids weren't listening, she leaned close. "They were burning Second Lifes in the park."

"Who?"

"I don't know. Some militia, maybe, but they just looked like regular people, from what I could tell. I didn't stick around or ask questions. There was so much hate there. The news is turning everybody against Second Lifes. I'm not staying here. I can't."

"Where will you go?"

She shook her head. "Anywhere. There has to be somewhere. Right?" She turned pleading eyes up to me. "Right? My Jidi… There has to be somewhere…"

I took her hands. "I'm going to give you a number. The woman on the other end, her name is Claire." Her eyes danced away toward where her children hid around the corner. I squeezed her hands to bring her attention back, dipping to catch her eye. "There is a group of us who look after one another. We are heading for the wastes."

"The wastes? I can't…"

"You can ride out the storm here. Stay hidden. Keep Jidi off the streets and his hair dyed, and hope the sniffers aren't tuned to find us. Maybe it will be fine. Maybe a different city will be better. At its core, this isn't about us. Second Lifes are a scapegoat, a distraction. Something other. Something easy to fear."

I held her eyes as she shifted nervously. "People are scared. Terrified. Not of us, but for their lives, and they are lashing out for some semblance of control. The city is volatile right now. The news is pumping in more fear and nervous energy to destabilize the situation and turn the population away from fighting the state. Soon we will all be fighting each other. People will be jumping at shadows. Accusing anybody of being a Second Life for any reason. So, maybe you will be able to ride it out. Maybe your family will go unnoticed. But maybe you won't." I straightened.

"Sara and I are going to take our chances in the wastes with the others. We stand a better chance together." I gave her hands a squeeze before dropping my hold. "What you saw today was horrible. Take a few deep breaths. Find yourself again. Then call Claire. Just get a feel for her. Do you think you can do that?"

She nodded.

I smiled, breathing deeply myself in the hopes that would help calm Farah. "Do you want me to help the boys pack?"

"No. No. We will be alright. Thank you, Ben."

She glanced at the door behind me. "Was there a reason you came over?"

"I just wanted to say thank you for the other night."

"We have to stick together."

I started to smile, then stopped, feeling the pull of my split lip. "You will fit right in with the Aunties if you choose to join us. Just be ready to go at a moment's notice."

30

My phone rang only once before I answered.

"Kea?"

"Take Sara and get out. Do it today."

"What?"

"You heard me. Get out of the city. Things are heating up. I know you have contacts. I know you were planning on going. So go. Tell your friends to move now."

"What's happening?"

"I don't know that I should tell you, Ben. You don't want to know."

"Tell me."

Kea growled to herself and I could picture her running her hand through her hair in frustration. Her tongue clicked several times as she considered. "Legislature."

I swallowed. I didn't know exactly what was going down, but I knew enough. There had been an undercurrent in Bekk's meeting, an increase in violence, and a line drawn in the sand. Kea had left enough of her breadcrumbs throughout our conversations in recent weeks that I could guess at her meaning.

"They are in session, Kea."

"Don't think I don't know that, Ben. I didn't plan this. This isn't… I'm trying to stop them. Take Sara. Get out of the city. Things are about to get bad."

"Please Kea. Reconsider. Come with us. I don't want to go without you."

"I know you don't want to. But you need to. I'm not leaving Zenith."

I had always known, but hearing the finality felt like a punch to the gut. "You won't be able to stop them," I said quietly.

Her words came in a resigned whisper. "Probably not, but I have to try. Call your friends. Get out."

I drew in a long breath, feeling too much like this was a farewell I wasn't ready for. "Okay. I love you, Kea."

"I love you too, Ben. Take care of Sara. Be safe out there."

I didn't waste any time in calling Claire.

"Claire. We have to go now."

She didn't question me. Didn't ask what I had heard. Didn't say anything but, "Okay. Today then. I'll get the word out." And that was it.

Sara was next. I sent a message to Emily in the hopes she would see it before I arrived at the school. I knew my sister wouldn't risk leaving Zenith. I had to hope that not being a Second Life and not being active on the front lines of the revolution would keep her and her family at least a little safer.

My thumb hesitated over the last number as I hurried for the bus stop. What did it matter anymore? Maybe we had taken a hiatus, but that didn't mean I didn't still care.

"Ben?" Rap sounded confused at my call. There had been no uncertainty in our final meeting. Still, she had answered.

"Stay in today, please."

She was quiet a moment. "What are you talking about, Ben?"

"Kea called me. I know what is going down. It's not right. You know it's not."

"Ben…"

"Destroying a symbol is one thing. This is not a symbol. This will stay with you forever. Just please. If you can't stop this, then stay in."

"I… I don't know what you are talking about…" But she did. Maybe we hadn't been together that long, but I had learned how she lied and how bad she was at it.

"Just stay in. Please."

She was quiet on her end. Down the street, the bus was pulling into view.

"I'm sorry we didn't work out, Rap. I think in a different time, in a different context, we could have been great."

"Wait. Ben? What are you doing?"

"Protecting Sara."

31

I looked back toward the city. Back toward the chaos unfolding. Already things were heating up. Unrest spreading like wildfire. It was the perfect time to slip away. To make a break for the wastes. There wasn't a promise of safety out there, but maybe it could be better. Maybe the Aunties were right. I had to hope they were.

My mind lingered on seeing Emily. Hoping it wouldn't be the last time. I'd held my sister for a long time. Promised I would find a way to stay in touch. In turn she had promised to keep her family in for as long as chaos reigned in the streets. Then I had taken Sara and ran.

We were close to the edge now, waiting for the rest of the group to arrive. Farah stood off to the side with her children, their bags packed into one of our many cars. I doubted the clunkers would make it far into the wastes, but every mile we could make it off our feet would be a boon. A warm wind blew in from the wastes, drawing my eyes away from the city. Instead of feeling unusual and sinister, it felt welcoming. As if the wilds knew our intent and sanctioned it wholly.

I looked at Claire and I saw a mix of disapproval and understanding there. She gave me a tight nod.

I stooped to meet Sara's eyes, my hands firm on her shoulders. "Sar, I need you to stay with the Aunties, alright?"

"I want to stay with you."

"The way I am going isn't safe. I need to know you will be safe. Stick to Auntie Claire like glue. Can you do that?"

She nodded, but a frown creased her lips. "Where are you going?"

"I am going after Auntie Kea."

Sara cringed. She had enough insight to know that wherever Kea had gone was somewhere she shouldn't be.

"I'll meet up with you outside the city."

She looked less certain. "If it's not safe for me to go with you, then how is it safe for you to go?"

"I'm not going to lie to you, kid. It's not." I patted her cheek. "But I need to try. I won't take any unnecessary risks."

"You can take one or two. It is Kea."

I chuckled, squeezing her shoulders before guiding her toward the waiting Second Lifes. Claire set a hand on Sara's shoulder, and Farah met my eye with a silent promise.

"I'll find you in the wastes," I promised them all. I didn't even question how. I knew that if I survived the night, I would find them. I would find Sara.

"Take care of yourself, Ben. We will keep an eye out for you." Claire said before turning to round up the group and get them moving.

We could all read the writing on the wall. The city was about to become a very dangerous place for those of us with the wrong sort of magic in our blood. Better to take our chances in the unknown.

***

Chaos reigned in Zenith. I hoped Emily and her family had made it home before everything fell apart. I hoped that the Aunties had escaped with Sara safely in tow. I hoped that nobody I loved was on the streets, but I knew better than that. Kea would never abandon Zenith.

The hill leading to the legislative building loomed ahead. Shades lined the roads leading into the government center, but I knew they were too late. These plans had been laid well before today. I hoped that rather than locking down the building and calling a shelter in place when attacks had cooked off around Zenith, the shades had evacuated the legislators. I hoped that maybe the body count wouldn't be as devastating as I knew it would be. From the number of shades lining the streets of the government complex, I knew that wouldn't be the case.

Protestors marched ahead of me, adding to the disorder of the moment. I shoved and elbowed through the crowd. A line up of press with their cameras and recording systems stood to the side, the shades corralling them along with the increasingly agitated protestors. There, strong shoulders and a shock of red hair. Kea, muscling her way to the front of the press line, trying to get any of the shades blocking their way to listen. I elbowed harder, trying to get to her.

The ground rattled, stilling the crowd.

I watched in horror as the legislative building seemed to rise and shudder, expanding outward as the walls exploded. I didn't even duck for cover. Didn't move from where my feet were rooted. The shaking of the blacktop beneath my feet and the warm rush of air from the blast whipping at my clothes couldn't best the weight of the stone in my stomach. People scattered as cement burst out toward the crowd with deadly force.

People hit the ground for cover. People were thrown to the ground by debris. To the right, another round of explosions sounded. Another government building went up in flames. No decision makers, just the workers that kept the lights on. To Bekk, maybe they were the same evil. More debris. More death. I fought to keep my feet as everybody beside me jostled to escape the devastation and the sudden outpouring of gunfire. I fought to get to where I had last seen Kea.

More explosions. More death. More screaming.

The streets of the government center were emptying, revealing the bodies left broken on the ground. Terrified and disorganized shades brandished their guns. I should have turned and fled, but I knew Kea wouldn't. I needed to find her.

Kea…

Nearby, a car sped by, leaving a trail of gunshots in its wake. Two shades dropped in their pursuit, struck. The car whizzed away.

Flames and debris were everywhere. More gunshots sounded. Small exchanges that ended quickly. There were screams and shouts and fires in every direction. Somehow, I found Kea laying among the rubble. She was still breathing. A flood of relief washed over me when I saw that rise and fall of her chest.

I pushed the debris off her and shook her shoulder gently.

"Kea. Come on. Wake up. You know I can't carry you."

Her eyelids fluttered, but that was all she gave me. I wrapped my arm around Kea's hips and hauled her along beside me. She was barely with it, but her feet plodded along unsteadily where I directed.

The legislative building lay in a fiery heap. Politicians and their security forces had been killed in mass during the explosion. The rows of shades forming a barricade now lay dead. The authorities wouldn't be long in arriving and they would come with guns drawn. We had to get away before we were trapped.

We staggered and stumbled between buildings. Crowds ran by, some in silent shock, some hysterical. Others clutching injuries or loved ones tight to their sides as they tried to put distance between them and the destruction.

We made it a few blocks, but a few blocks didn't buy us any safety. There was no calm in Zenith.

I hit the ground when another volley of gunfire sounded. Cars sped by, and people holding guns took off in every direction. Searing pain tore through my shoulder, and I clutched at the spot while I lay protectively over Kea.

When the cars and the gunfire passed again, I lifted off of Kea. She didn't move. Her muscular back no longer shifted with breath and life. A fresh wash of blood bloomed across her back. I rolled her onto my legs, holding her tight. She was too still. Her face was slack. None of the joy of life and determination I was so used to seeing in her features was gone.

Did I feel a pull? A warm wind? Any hint of magic in the air? Anything?

My eyes pressed closed, and I focused, trying to will some hint of magic into the air.

I felt nothing. Only hollow.

We had grown up together. We had cried on each other's shoulders. We had been there for each other at every turn. I owed her my life.

I sat for so long with her. I waited. I hoped, even though I knew it was pointless. Kea was gone. I had to keep going and I couldn't bring her with me.

I set her in a position I hoped was comfortable. Her face was etched into my memory. I would never forget her. I stroked her cheek, then stood and started toward the wastes.

My phone buzzed and my mind went instantly to Sara. What else could go wrong tonight?

I glanced at the text.

Rap: *I stayed in tonight.*

It was as much an apology as it was a statement of me being right.

I looked at the blood on my hands, thought of Kea's body lifeless across my legs, then threw my phone into the trash and ran to find my daughter.

Thank you for reading A Second Life Worth Living!

If you enjoyed this story, please leave a rating and a short review (just a few words are more than enough) to help others find my work.

Check out my website to join my newsletter, receive updates on my writing progress, and learn about my upcoming releases.
KarenLuciaAuthor.com

BOOKS BY KAREN LUCIA

Landbringer

THE WARRIORS OF HELSVERN SERIES:
The Golden Valia
Daughter of Helsvern
Son of Helsvern

FROM EARTH TO THE UNKNOWN:
The Divide
Funeral Singer
Blackburn Station
Greystone Alliance

ACKNOWLEDGEMENTS

Thank you to my family and friends! Your constant support and willingness to read my work before it is fully refined keeps me going. Here's another one for you. Hope it isn't too dark.

ABOUT THE AUTHOR

Karen is a Minneapolis, Minnesota based author. During the long, cold winters she learned the value of a good story, good friends, and a strong internet connection. Writing has been a passion project for her since childhood. It took that passion, her love of stories, and her friends to get her books out into the world.